Sex and Death, I Suppose

Sex and Death, I Suppose

Michael Colonnese

Oak Tree Press  Taylorville, IL

Oak Tree Press

Oak Tree Press books may be purchased for educational, business or sales promotional purposes. Contact Publisher for quantity discounts.

First Edition, January 2011

Cover Design by Pat Roberts

978-1-61009-002-5
LCCN 2010933219

For Robin

Acknowledgments

I gratefully acknowledge the North Carolina Arts Council's Fayetteville and Cumberland County Regional Artist Program, the residency program at Vermont Studio Center, the Eastern Frontier Foundation's Norton's Island residency program, Methodist University's sabbatical program, and the residency program at the Weymouth Center for the Arts and Humanities, all of which were instrumental in providing time and space to write this novel. I'd also like to express my appreciation to Jeannie Denman, who typed an early draft, to Pat Roberts, for her original cover design, and to Billie Johnson of Oak Tree Press for her editorial expertise. Finally, I'd like to thank my wife, Robin Greene, for encouraging me to keep writing. Without her support, this novel might never have been completed.

CHAPTER *1*

Wondering if needing to smoke grass before breakfast to keep from swilling a six-pack before noon meant that I'd fallen off the wagon again and how I'd explain that to Lorrie, my girlfriend and psycho-analyst, I crimped the end of my smoldering joint and swallowed the tiny roach. I'd been refusing to think of myself as a private investigator all morning—which wasn't easy. Giving up detective work was like trying to stay sober. I kept feeling like I was missing something important, a familiar self perhaps, some unnecessary crutch I'd come to rely on.

Alone in the third-floor office I shared with recently silenced automatic dialing machines once owned by a for-profit-non-profit that ran telemarketing scams involving bone cancer in little kids, I studied my reflection in a metal-framed window. I didn't like what I saw. An overweight guy with a long salt-and-pepper hair was float-ing like a debauched cherub in a cloud of sweetish smoke. Slowly, almost like it belonged to somebody else, I watched my arm snake for the phone. I dialed Jerry East, a real estate guy I knew.

"Realty-World—East and Associates."

"Jerry," I said. "Answering your own line?"

"Peter," he said, imitation jolly. "How's the detective business?"

"Face down in the sewage," I said. "You listing many houses?"

"So long as interest rates hold steady, I can't complain."

"Staying that busy, huh?"

Jerry sighed deeply, a long whoosh of exhaustion with sorrow for the planet in it. I liked Jerry East better than I liked most people, but he was almost as much of a failure as I was and had fewer good years left to turn things around. Still, we understood each other on some superficial level and there were plenty of worse ways to make a living in Bridgewater.

"Actually, I'm working with this yuppie who wants to build a six-bay car wash—he walked in off the street—and I'll be damned if I can find him a commercial lot at anything like a reasonable price."

"Maybe I can help," I said and coughed up my last hit.

"Help?" Jerry said. "Downtown planning commission thinks they can limit commercial zoning. Half the city council owns an interest in the suburban malls, and meanwhile all those contaminated factories sit vacant with broken windows."

"I know," I said. And I did.

"Well, since you obviously got nothing better to do, why not beat the bushes? I'd pay you a finder's fee."

"Maybe," I said, already so bored by Jerry's pull-yourself-up-by-your-bootstraps bullshit that I was nearly half asleep, although there was actually one vacant and potentially-for-sale house in a new commercial zone that I knew about. A long, long shot, but so what?

"Well," I said, "hang tough, Jerry. Things will pick up."

"Right," he said. "And, actually, my residential sales ain't been bad. You take care now."

I hung up, wondering if I tended to surround myself with losers or whether there were simply a lot of losers around. In a way, I supposed I was more fortunate than most. Jerry and I were survivors of the post-love generation, the one that had come of age in the late nineteen-seventies— back when the hash-pipe dream of a counter-culture had finally quit attempting to expand like a helium balloon and instead simply lay there as limp as a discarded condom.

Nowadays, the burden of commerce was surely too much with us although, except for rent, food, beer, whiskey, vodka, grass, cocaine, gasoline, and the high-risk rates I paid for car insurance, I didn't have many fixed expenses. I was still my own boss, and I had a new digital camera—just in case I needed a snapshot of somebody's unfaithful spouse.

For the last six months or so, I'd been earning a few supplemental dollars as a real estate photographer, taking photos of new listings for the county MLS Service. When I found employment as a detective I mostly did divorce work, but lately it seemed like every out-of-work private investigator in town was working divorces on speculation, videotaping the comings and goings at the by-the-hour roach motels, hoping to capture some solid citizen doing the extracurricular nasty.

Anyway, that was how bad it could get, and I hopefully wouldn't get desperate enough to stoop to that kind of private detection for at least another week. If my drinking got out of hand, I could always find an AA meeting, and if Jerry East was right about one thing—I had nothing better to do.

CHAPTER 2

It was an ancient, Great-Gatsby monstrosity, an estate-sized white-pillared mansion set back from the root-buckled sidewalk of upper Main Street and surrounded by dying privet hedges and the rusty lance points of an iron fence. On a pad behind the privacy hedges sat a black Olds 88 with two flat tires. Up close, the house looked to be in rotten shape—so bad I revised the sales price downward and had Jerry East list it for sale as-is—this entire complicated transaction happening entirely in my head. The clapboard siding had needed paint for so long that by now only vinyl siding could cover the decay—not that the rot mattered because they'd bulldoze the place.

As any of the imaginary associates at Jerry East's struggling Realty World franchise could tell you—knowledge they'd somehow managed to acquire without ever once attempting a deconstructive literary analysis of single repetitive sentence by Gertrude Stein (location, location, location)—this was a vacant house on a commercially zoned lot in the once-prestigious North End, a neighborhood some still called Doctor's Row. Thirty or forty years ago, nearly all of the houses here had belonged to physicians—mainly successful surgeons—who'd once wanted large homes within easy walking distance of Saint Sebastian's Hospital.

But that was then. Lately, there'd been a debate in the Bridgewater city council over the wisdom of operating a publicly-owned health-care facility—because nowadays Saint Sebastian's was basically a charity hospital that needed to be city subsidized, and it operated at a considerable loss. In fact, a one-block area adjacent to the hospital had recently been rezoned as *mixed-use commercial* so as to permit the operation of a privately-owned AIDS Hospice and a new, for-profit substance-abuse clinic, each designed to complement the taxpayer-funded methadone distribution center and a 24-hour emergency-room that Saint Sebastian's continued to staff.

This rezoning was a deliberately under-publicized fact that not everyone would know about—not even every commercial real estate agent. But some of the druggie crowd with whom I'd gone to high school were middle-aged junkies or alcoholics now, or else ex-junkies or ex-alcoholics, and having a passing interest in such facilities myself—seeing as how I was currently being court supervised by Lorrie after three DUI arrests and one plea-bargained-down conviction in the last six months—I had followed the protracted zoning battle rather closely.

I parked my ancient Escort in the street, listened to it cough and stutter for a minute after I cut the ignition, then left it parked under a dying oak, unlocked in a cloud of black exhaust, figuring it was too old and shitty a car to tempt anyone to steal it. I made my way to the driveway gate. If I weren't paranoid enough to mind the stares from the drug-dealers down the block, a half-dozen loitering teenagers in sagging jeans that showcased their designer boxer shorts and two-hundred-dollar athletic shoes, in some ways it still didn't seem like all that bad a neighborhood.

The gate's rusty hinges whined under my hand as I moved it to one side. I climbed six unpainted steps to a rotting porch—hoping to survey the subject property, as Jerry East would say. The porch roof was obviously leaking, the floorboards sagging and slippery with a greenish slime, and I could see a dozen or so yellow, rolled-in-plastic newspapers molding away by the front door. They had been there long enough to soak up rainwater despite their plastic wrappers, and the smell of the place got worse and worse the closer to the door I got. I knocked twice—why I didn't know—because by then it was clear that the premises weren't occupied, and when nobody answered I tried the knob. The door swung open, and I saw the body lying there—face down in the foyer—and understood pretty quickly what had kept prospective looters at bay.

I gagged and covered my mouth to keep from puking. I'd seen dead bodies before. Once I'd even identified a thirteen-year-old runaway I'd been hired to look for—and had unfortunately found at the county morgue. But those were the bodies of the recently dead, and this one had been there for so long that it had stiffened and relaxed and swollen and burst and dried again and was slowly becoming one with the parquet. I also guessed that this had once been a middle-aged male's body because it was wearing thin nylon socks and men's brown leather wing-tips with fancy punch work around the toe-box, but the rest of his legs were hairless and naked, and the genitals and face were gone and looked like they'd been gnawed. Rats, I supposed.

But I couldn't quit staring and couldn't think what to do, and it sure didn't look like I'd get Jerry East a commercial listing out of it. If I'd had any sense, I'd have wiped the door knob clean and run, but a part of me was curious and obviously stuck in the rut of thinking of myself as a private detective because I decided to snoop around.

I stepped over the body and made my way through the area downstairs. In the kitchen, I saw a coffee cup in the sink and a dirty plastic drain board with nothing on it, and some blackened slabs of toast sticking out of an old-fashioned toaster on the counter. I made sure not to touch anything or leave any fingerprints. The refrigerator door was open and smelled almost as bad as the body, but the power was off and, except for a glass of yellow milk partially fermented into scummy cheese, the gray metal racks were empty.

A carpeted stairway led upstairs off the kitchen and I climbed, watching my feet and not touching the banister. The upstairs rooms looked mostly empty, with wide board floors swept clean—all except for one black-and-white art-deco tiled bathroom where a rusty can of shaving cream and an undersized bar of hard yellow motel soap rested on a corroded chrome rack by the sink. On a whim, I checked the bedroom closet, nudging an accordion-paneled door open with my foot. A few shirts and a baggy gray suit still hung on wire hangers, and a small old-fashioned valise—a dust-covered cardboard satchel with red leather trim—rested on the closet floor.

I hesitated, then bent and laid the satchel flat and flipped the latches. In film noir, small suitcases were nearly always filled with unmarked but banded stacks of stolen money, and I was playing private detective again. But no sooner had I gotten it open than I really wished I hadn't.

Because at first what I thought I'd discovered was a collection of dried flowers. Small translucent yellow and pink petals started spilling out—as if from a float in some ancient California rose-bowl parade. But I was three thousand miles from California and where the idea of rose petals had come from was clearly the land of denial. Because those funny looking flower petals weren't petals at all. They were scraps of human skin—or rather dried human breast nipples attached to scraps of skin—some of them a little pinkish where blood had caked and dried.

I wanted out. I nudged the nipples that had fallen out of the satchel back inside the closet with my shoe and closed the dis-colored brass latches and wiped everything I'd touched with my shirttails. A few minutes earlier I'd been entertaining vague notions of acting like a responsible citizen and letting the cops know about the body downstairs when I was done with my snooping around, but now there was all manner of legal shit I didn't want to be involved with, and mutilated human body parts certainly qualified as something best avoided. Besides, I was no longer certain that it was rats that had gotten to the man downstairs.

I headed for the stairs and started down about as fast as I could go, but stopped when I saw the cash pinned to a corkboard on the side wall of the landing. Some detective. How I'd missed it going up I didn't know, but it was certainly there and right at eyeball height. A handwritten note and a short stack of Ben Franklins—these fastened to the corkboard by a huge red plastic pushpin. I read the note:

> Diedre,
>
> Don't forget to leave the money for Greenwood once his services have been rendered
>
> —Sue

I pulled the push pin, pocketed the cash, pushed the pin back though the note and into the crumbly corkboard, and immediately slid my hand back into my pocket to finger the money again. Fifty-dollar bills—four of them. I guessed Diedre had never gotten Sue's message, or else Greenwood had never rendered his services. Or, if the guy on the floor downstairs was Greenwood, he obviously didn't need the payment. Anyway, I wasn't about to leave it hanging there for Bridgewater's finest to appropriate or for some adventurous neighborhood junkie to plunder. All this by way of justifying a common burglary.

In fact, once I had wiped the doorknob and was out of the front yard and then back in my rattletrap car and headed down the road, I began to feel pretty good. Joyful, almost manic. A golden oldie about a mystery ship came on the car's radio, and I started to sing along.

It was a pretty cold-blooded way to behave, but I suddenly felt like I'd been rewarded by fate for being exactly who I was. Two hundred bucks richer and happy to be alive. I decided I would take Lorrie somewhere nice to eat tonight. My treat for a change. The fancy Mexican place maybe.

CHAPTER 3

"Two for the back room," I said, and held up two fingers, flashing a peace sign at the pair of tall golden blondes who worked as greeters in La Hacienda. Sisters they were, twenty-something identical twins. They were wearing white, low-cut peasant blouses and long green shirts with side slits that showcased their chemically tanned thighs. I'd often wondered what the golden twins were being paid to work weekends, and how much extra business they attracted simply by existing as embodiments of male fantasy—for clearly neither of them could possibly be as shallow as she seemed.

"Right this way," one said, and swished away with two big plastic menus. I tried to stifle a hard-on by telling myself it was simply her job. Meanwhile, the other pretty twin grimaced like it hurt her tiny brain to concentrate and made red Xs on a white clipboard with an erasable marker.

"Put us in a booth," I said, and followed Lorrie, who followed her. In her own quiet way Lorrie was as attractive as either of the blonds, although she was older—twenty-nine last month, and her sexuality far less obvious. A skinny black girl wearing tight-black jeans and Birkenstock sandals and almost no makeup, her frizzy brown hair done up in cornrows. She wouldn't normally be noticed in a crowd, but because she with me, a middle-aged white guy, I could tell we were getting a little extra attention—people trying not to stare. Only fifty miles from Manhattan, but Bridgewater was still pretty backward when it came to pretending to ignore interracial couples.

"Will this be all right?"

"Fine," I said and slid in opposite Lorrie. A blond twin passed each of us a menu. All the tables were thick slabs of polyurethane-coated pine with high-backed bench seats covered in brown vinyl. The decor was basically old advertising signs and pastel-colored sombreros mounted high on stucco walls where the rough-textured surface could thorn out an eyeball if somebody got drunk enough to stumble against it.

On every table was a gas-fueled lantern in an iron holder. The menu twin leaned over to light it in a way that made me wonder if she was deliberately giving me a peek at her silicon-swelled breasts. I realized once again that I entertained hopes that Lorrie and I would be doing it tonight if we could make it though the entire meal and our usual preliminaries without a fight.

"Drinks before dinner?" the blond said, waving away smoke from the long match.

Lorrie gave me a look.

"A big glass of ice water," I said.

"A wedge of lemon in my water, please," said Lorrie, "and I'll have decaf after dinner."

"Martinque will be your server," the menu twin said, and went away.

"So, how was work?" I asked, once the greeter had left us in peace.

"Don't ask, baby," Lorrie said softly. "My schizophrenic mailman was hallucinating that he had rabies again—I had to call all over town to find someone to write him a script. Our house psychiatrist was all tied up in court with my pedophile, lullabying the jury at a thousand per diem. Then my epileptic housewife had a grand-mal in group, and by the time I got everybody settled down and resched-uled for next week, I ended up skipping lunch so I'm famished."

All this was actually Lorrie's way of being simultaneously candid and professionally discrete. As usual, she gossiped about clients and colleagues shamelessly, but seldom if ever by name. It was always my schizophrenic mailman, or my transsexual cop, or my manic depressive secretary. Lorrie had been working as a therapist for so long that her vocabulary had taken on a kind of possessiveness that was vaguely contagious. Sometimes I'd even felt jealous, almost like I knew these people and suspected deep down I was sicker than they were and had a better claim to Lorrie's time.

Often I'd even wondered what she had told them about me, because, professionally speaking, if anybody knew how terribly fragile my life and finances were, Lorrie surely did. Not that I was blaming her for my problems, but Lorrie worked in mental health, and back when we'd first made my post-DUI plea-bargained therapy sessions more interesting by becoming lovers, she would sometimes refer a patient to me, usually some troubled soul whose daily functionality was far more compromised than my own.

But even back then, in the sub-rosa dawn of our sexual intimacy, when Lorrie still didn't know me very well and was still sending an occasional loser my way, most of her referrals had been under-age welfare mothers, and more often than not I'd been sent chasing after some not-all-that-hard-to-find paternity-suit boyfriend who had gotten behind on his child support. More than once I'd ended up confronting some blue-collar slob who was barely making ends meet. I'd charge into his pathetic existence, threaten him with family court, tell him he was looking at garnisheed wages and ruinous legal fees, and he'd ordinarily cough up a couple of hundred bucks, of which, for my discrete professional investigative services, I'd take a fifty percent cut. Sometimes, though, if the situation looked hopeless enough, I'd find that in good conscience I couldn't keep the fifty percent, and once or twice I'd ended up adding a few dollars of my own, making small donations so some impoverished teenage mom could feed her hungry kids.

According to Lorrie, she'd quit referring such clients to me because this was an unhealthy psychological pattern that fostered emotional dependency, and was, consequently, no way for me to run my detective business, especially seeing as how I already had weak ego boundaries—as a result of being deserted by my own mother back when I was a boy, and that in my intimate relationships with women I was unconsciously seeking some kind of external approval to make up for the anger and guilt I felt for feeling unlovable. I certainly understood all that crap, and reluctantly agreed that about half of it made sense, but I also knew that, like most of Lorrie's psychoanalytic explanations, this one was overly complicated; my wiring was more direct. Despite solid evidence to the contrary, I'd persisted in thinking of myself as a guy with a big heart.

"And how was your workday, Pete?" Lorrie asked, and squeezed my hand, but the question suddenly seemed so obligatory that I hesitated before answering. When Lorrie started being gentle with me something bad was usually brewing. But perhaps some repressed traumatic memory was making me overly sensitive to nuance.

"Slow," I lied. "I got to feeling desperate, so I called Jerry East. I'm thinking of trying to sell real estate for him."

"I'm not sure that would be wise, Peter."

"I'm keeping my options open."

"But the income's inherently unstable. You know how you get."

"Then you'd better start sending me some new clients—because I know about unstable and I need to pay my rent."

I watched her face as she considered this suggestion, probably trying to decide if I was yanking her chain.

"Actually, I mentioned your name to someone earlier this week," she said softly. "You could actually help her."

"Yeah? How?"

"Now don't get paranoid. Her name is Mrs. Elizabeth McLean and she's an eighty-five-year old widow. Her late husband was once the mayor of Bridgewater—and he died under mysterious circumstances. I passed her your business card. She's a functional neurotic, but her real problem isn't emotional. More like she needs help gathering information if she's ever to put old ghosts to rest. Basically, she doesn't know who to trust."

I smiled, imagining myself for a minute as somebody anybody could trust.

"Really Peter," Lorrie said. "She could use a friend."

"I'm not in the sympathy business," I said. "Besides, if she's really who you say she is, she's rich."

An overweight waitress in a tight T-shirt and a sombrero saun-tered over with two large glasses of water. She set them down. She looked Flemish or maybe Polish and spoke with a slight accent. For some reason I wondered if she shaved her underarms and decided she didn't.

"I'm Martinique," she said. "Have we decided or do we need another minute."

"Are we ready?" I asked.

"White guys are always ready," Lorrie said, and winked as if she could read my mind. "Or maybe that's an ugly myth."

"I'll have the fajitas trio, and a double-fried chimichunga with an extra side of sour cream," I said.

Lorrie smiled and said softly, " Peter, I thought you were dieting?"

"I haven't eaten anything all day," I said.

"That's no way to diet."

"You diet your way, I'll diet mine," I said.

"And we'd like..."said Martinique.

"I'll have the three-bean Mexican salad," Lorrie said. Rubbing it in because she was also a vegetarian.

"Coming up," said Martinique.

"You know, we've been arguing quite a lot lately, Peter," Lorrie said, starting in again just as soon as Martinique had left.

"Jesus, I'll eat whatever you say!"

"It's not just that," Lorrie said. "People around the office have been starting to gossip. And I suppose I've been feeling ambivalent lately. I mean…my colleagues aren't idiots, and dating a client is clearly a no-no."

I hesitated. "A no-no, huh? What kind of baby-talk crap is that?"

"Just that either you should find another therapist soon or we should stop seeing each other for a while."

I didn't say anything at first—I was dumbstruck. I hadn't been expecting this kind of go-round tonight. It was hard work to keep my lower jaw from falling open. "Like you think maybe I don't realize I'm porking up?"I said. "Grant me some self awareness."

"That's really not the point."

"Does everything have a point?"

"Obviously and obviously not."

But our entire meal was already spoiled, tensions popping and sizzling between us like my fajitas, until finally we were lingering over some syrupy flan and decaf, and I began to tune Lorrie out. I obviously needed to rethink my life again. I wasn't exactly feeling as bad as this morning because I was suddenly too numb for that, but the manic high I'd experienced after pocketing the two hundred dollars had worn pretty thin. If anything, I felt the way I felt whenever I ordered the veal while eating with Lorrie in my favorite Italian place. Sort of guilty, sort of not, and sort of glad I wasn't a baby cow.

"Spell it out," I said. "You want to dump me or what?"

"Did I say that, baby?"

I took a deep breath, trying to put things in perspective. "Then apropos of nothing, can I ask you a simple professional question? As my therapist, I mean?"

Lorrie nodded and put both fists under her chin, deceptively innocent and sweet.

"What's the explanation for sexual mutilation?"

"And vat has been mutilated, baby?" she asked softly in her best Austrian accent.

"Say the severing of a body part?"

"Ah," she said. And then, "Vat exactly are ve missing, baby?"

When I gave her a nasty look, she started laughing. I supposed that in another context I might have thought it funny too, but it was a little too close to home.

"Let's say a set of breast nipples," I said.

That got her attention. "Well, obviously there's a lot of unconscious anger. Mother, sister, something pretty primal."

"Obviously," I said.

"This one of your nightmares, Peter?" she asked softly, concerned now but trying not to show it.

"You wish?" I said.

"Obviously not," she said, annoyed.

"Sorry," I said. "I'm a little on edge."

"What about?"

"Money, money, money, money," I said. "Money and its relationship to sex. Money and its relationship to love. Money and its relationship to happiness."

"If you're worried about money, you should see Mrs. McLean," Lorrie mused. "She does need to hire someone, and she might be too afraid to reach out."

"Everybody's afraid of something," I said.

"If I give you Mrs. McLean's number, would you promise to call her?"

I shrugged, and Lorrie gave me a look. She knew I hated talking on the phone with people I didn't know, although I didn't have a problem confronting strangers in person.

"You know, Peter," Lorrie said, and the tone of her voice told me I was in for a lecture. "If your detective business isn't working out, you could go back to college. I mean, a person of your intelligence..."

"By staying chronically under-employed, I'm expressing my solidarity with the underclass."

"Absolute bullshit," Lorrie said, but I'd managed to make her smile.

"Or maybe I'm just expressing the conviction that things are tough all over."

Lorrie laughed again, but it wasn't a real laugh and she was done being distracted. "So whose nipples are missing?"

CHAPTER 4

I woke up in a sweat. My underarms reeked of musk, and my groin
of generic spermicide, and the waterbed itself smelled ever-so-
faintly of over-chlorinated water and heated plastic, so it was as if
someone had stuffed road-kill under Lorrie's black silk sheets. Gray
light was beginning to rise with the day outside. After dinner and
the check and some red-and-white peppermints in the Mexican
place, Lorrie and I had sort of agreed that maybe it was time to let
our relationship chill so as to avoid making rash decisions about
our future. Very civilized and mature behavior.

So the new day began, and before I thought of anything else, even
before rubbing yellow grit from my eyes, I lay there smelling the imperfect smells of this imperfect world and reached across the bed to
run my hand ever-so-gently just above Lorrie's naked rump. I could
feel heat rising from her firm, aerobics-every-other-day body, but I
didn't quite make contact, didn't quite touch her skin. Except in the
dead of winter I usually slept bare-assed myself, but Lorrie always
slept naked, and I tried to take a kind of comfort in the hard-core fact
that this brown beauty and I were still sharing her big waterbed.

She stirred in her sleep—punched the king-sized pillow twice,
but didn't wake. Last night, I'd had to give her a long backrub in
order to help her relax. We'd made love finally, and she'd seemed to
enjoy herself—but it had somehow seemed more like the casual
coupling of strangers.

Lately, I'd begun to wonder if the pre-coital tensions that seemed to regenerate like a Phoenix between Lorrie and me weren't a side effect of some cruel battery of personality tests that she was secretly forcing me to take. Periodically announcing that our relationship was in trouble so as to test my emotional stability. Or else some kind of kinky foreplay she needed to get off.

Or maybe it wasn't nearly that complicated. Maybe Lorrie simply needed to feel wanted by somebody very, very insecure. That would fit the profile for a working psychoanalyst, and Lorrie was certainly at her cock-teasing best when it came to provoking my complicated emotions. Psycho-sexually speaking, she had me tied up in square knots. Neither of us had made any demands on the other to be monogamous, and while I'd occasionally confessed to having other lovers, Lorrie never did. Probably because she knew it would make me sick with jealousy and had decided to spare me. I was fairly sure she had other sexual partners—there were any number of male graduate-school friends she sometimes visited for long weekends, but, as for that, most of them looked a little limp-wristed to me—gay or bisexual. What really went on during her little excursions, I couldn't force myself to ask. Consequently, we'd established a solid basis for trust in that regard—my ignorance and her discretion.

Transference and counter transference and all that silly complicated shit aside, Lorrie's professional success as a therapist for middle-aged white guys like me—or so she claimed—was a natural consequence a forbidden-fruit dynamic that itself resulted from her being an Afro-American feminist, although I'd sometimes chided her that it probably had more to do with her looking gentle and non-threatening, a slender, brown babe from a wealthy, boarding-school background.

But Lorrie would get her all-cotton bikini-cut panties in a wad if I said honest stuff like that. So usually I deferred and let her think what she wanted. She was still, after all, my court-appointed therapist, and I did occasionally suffer from the unhealthy desire to make a romantic fairytale out of things. In my better and more manic moments, the absolute wonder and arbitrary joy of simply being alive at all—well, it could sometimes overwhelm me. At such moments the world seemed to have a kind of unity, to make a kind of sense. In my more sober and reflective moods, however, I'd wondered if the need for a coherent narrative wasn't encoded in the human genome. Because like every other lost soul on the planet I was always expecting the facts to add up, to symbolize, to quit jumping around like poisoned fleas on a poodle and stand quietly in line— which is why people hired psychoanalysts or private detectives.

Thankfully, I hadn't made a complete ass of myself last night by once again asking Lorrie to marry me. Not that I hadn't been tempted. Fortunately, after lovemaking, I'd been too exhausted to communicate and simply rolled over to my side of the bed and untangled the sheets and slept. I'd dreamed that I was a man without a face, wandering around a deserted house with a matched pair of empty suitcases. Of course, one of problems with dating a shrink was you started to understand this sort of thing even before you told it to anyone, and you had to decide on a need-to-know basis exactly what and how much you were willing to reveal.

Because, of course, I'd lied to Lorrie last night, refusing to answer her question about the missing nipples, saying it was something I'd heard on my police scanner. Predictably, Lorrie hadn't believed me and insisted it was stupid to keep secrets from your therapist who, after all, you were supposed to trust implicitly. Although why it was stupid to be reticent if she didn't love me unconditionally—that I didn't ask.

I slipped quietly out of bed and poured bottled water into Lorrie's Mr. Coffee and took a short dip in her whirlpool tub and wrapped a towel around my waist to go downstairs and collect her morning paper. I shed the towel afterwards and walked around her apartment naked while Lorrie slept on and on. I didn't feel like talking anyway. I sipped her shade-grown, fair-trade coffee and fixed myself a bowl of her raspberry granola with organic no-fat milk. I often did my best thinking in the morning. It certainly didn't look like my leap into real estate referrals was fated to be my next career move. But in some strange way I felt okay. I felt like a minor character in a Russian novel where I just been condemned to death as a revolutionary but had been granted a reprieve at the last moment just before the firing squad let loose a volley.

Then I opened the morning's Bridgewater *Telegram*, read yesterday's crime report, and felt my heart skip a beat or two and shudder against my ribs.

Missing Woman Becomes Murder Victim

Bridgewater Police are now investigating a violent assault by a killer they're calling the Exacto-Knife rapist. The mutilated body of Diedre Richmond, 27, a 2nd grade teacher at Columbus Elementary, was discovered last night in a seldom-used utility closet in the parking garage of the Bridgewater Shopping Plaza.

Police acknowledged that the unclad body was partially decomposed but would confirm only that the victim's upper torso had been slashed by an assailant. Richmond had been reported missing when she failed to report to work. Divorced, she was the mother of two sons, ages 9 and 7, currently in the custody of Children's Protective Services.

I read the article; then I read it again. And then I felt disgusted with myself and irrationally guilty that I hadn't immediately reported what I'd seen at that abandoned mansion—although nothing I might have done could have prevented a murder that had obviously happened some time ago.

It was a sign of our terrible times, I supposed, that an at-large sex killer in a violent rape and murder case had only merited four sentences in the Bridgewater Telegram. For in spite of its being rather abominably written, the story had contained enough detail to send my blood pressure soaring—not a good thing with strokes and heart disease in my family history. I obviously possessed information that the cops ought to have. It was one thing to walk away from an anonymous dead body and a collection of nipples, but if some psychopath was still out there, killing innocent young mothers and collecting souvenirs, I supposed I felt obligated to tell somebody what I knew.

I decided to take the path of least resistance. I'd call the cops from a public phone and get things off my chest, disguise my voice and keep it short and sweet. I got dressed quickly and left a cryptic note on the kitchen counter for Lorrie, telling her I had an early morning appointment. I strolled down the block to find a pay phone. These days, it seemed like everybody carried a cell, and there simply weren't that many pay phones left around. Finally, I did find one, but unfortunately, it had been vandalized: the metal cord had been severed and the receiver was missing. As usual, nothing was easy.

Haunted by death and consequently annoyed, I walked back down the street to collect my Escort, got in, started the engine, warmed it for a minute so it wouldn't stall, then drove slowly into downtown Bridgewater with black smoke still pouring from my tailpipes because the engine needed new rings. I kept looking for another pay phone and someplace I could park.

One of the little things that had killed off downtown shopping was the lack of metered parking spaces. Twenty or so years ago, the Bridgewater Shopping Plaza had been built, mostly with federal loans, in an abortive attempt to jump-start urban renewal, but the attached eight-story parking garage they'd constructed cost six dollars an hour to use and had smelled like a latrine almost from day one. Bridgewater locals called it the Bat Cave, mainly because it was gloomy and attracted human vermin—as that nippleless school teacher had no doubt discovered. Consequently, the shopping plaza had never quite caught on. Most shoppers preferred the relative safety of the suburban malls, and the Bat Cave normally had its relatively expensive parking spots available, so I finally gave up looking for a metered space on the street and let an automated parking-stub machine raise the arm and let me in.

But parking in the Bat Cave was in short supply today. I found the ground floor and second level filled and the third-level access ramp crossed by yellow crime-scene tape. I pounded the Escort's steering wheel with my fist and turned around. I was wasting my entire day. Finally, I grabbed a handicapped space on the second level—one of four empties in a row, thinking I'd only be a minute.

I parked and locked my Escort for fear some wino would piss in it, and ran across the concrete bridge that connected the garage with the mall.

By a toy emporium inside the plaza, I finally found a working pay phone, so I dialed 911 and stuck my finger in one ear. A couple of giggling pre-teens came strolling by—adolescent girls with partially shaved heads and wearing a lot of leather, holding hands, doing their junior-high rebellion thing, wagging their pointy pink tongues and touching them together when they saw me staring—as if they could shock me. Both of them had tiny nose rings and zircons in their teeth. Musac was in the air—static electricity and a string quartet version of "Born in the USA." The operator came on. I made my voice sound high and squeaky. "Police Department, please."

"Is this an emergency?"

I had to think about it. "Well, I'd like to report a mutilated body."

I heard a clicking sound. "Police. Emergency."

"3134 Main Street. Dead guy on the floor downstairs," I said. "And better check the upstairs closet."

"Units are rolling. Your name, please?"

I hung up.

CHAPTER **5**

A young female cop was writing me a ticket when I got back to my car. A knockout redhead who looked fresh out of the police academy, still girlishly prim in a starched blue blouse and navy polyester slacks. She had short curly hair, freckles across her nose and cheeks, pale blue eyes, and shiny handcuffs. An unscratched ebony nightstick dangled from her wide black plastic belt like a dildo. I walked right up and smiled what I hoped was a seductively disarming smile, but which probably looked like a leer.

"I was just going to move it," I said, jingling my keys, hoping that I could bullshit my way out of a ticket, or maybe also to see if there were anything about her worth knowing.

"You the owner of this vehicle?"

"That's me," I said, and grinned even wider.

"You're occupying a handicapped space, Sir."

"I know, I know, but I needed to use the phone. The other three handicapped spaces were empty—still are, if you noticed."

"I noticed," she said, but she continued to scribble on her triple-carbon pad.

"Look, officer, I'm paying six bucks to park and there weren't any other spaces. The cops have the upper levels blocked off."

She didn't even look up.

"What about letting me off with a warning? I wasn't parked illegally any more than ten minutes."

"I've already called for a tow truck."

"I'll move it!"

She tore off the ticket. "Sign at the X to acknowledge receipt. Officially your vehicle's been impounded, but the tow-truck driver may let you drive it away if you can negotiate his dispatch fee."

I took the proffered pen and casually signed her pad. "So how much is the dispatch fee these days?"

"I believe it's a one-hundred dollar minimum, Sir. And there could also be a storage charge. Plus this ticket's going to cost you another hundred."

I hesitated. If I hadn't stolen two hundred dollars yesterday, I'd have felt royally screwed, but I hadn't carried that money around quite long enough to feel like it was entirely mine and was sort of disposed to write off a traffic ticket as the karmic cost of doing business, but then again, there'd been plenty of times lately when a two-hundred dollar fine would have just about broken me. If I were going end up paying the ticket anyway, I might as well make a rookie cop feel shitty. In short, I was royally pissed off and ready to give her a hard time.

I smiled vaguely and whispered, "And what of kickback do you imagine somebody would have to promise to get that kind of towing contract from the city?"

"I really wouldn't know anything about that, Sir."

"Yeah," I said, "A dirty business. The traffic cop business. With everybody on the take, I mean."

She grimaced, letting me know I'd already said something to punch though her reserve.

"I don't appreciate that remark, Sir. My father happens to be a career police officer—thirty years on the force. And two older brothers are also policemen. No one in our family is in any sense dishonest."

"Yeah," I said thoughtfully. "Then maybe it's me. Maybe I'm being too a little too cynical."

"Perhaps 'cynical' is one word for what you're being," she said softly.

"So what's the family name of this incorruptible bunch of cops?"

"O'Donald, Sally. Badge number OZ8645. It's on your ticket."

"Irish girl, huh? Bet old' honest Dad busted his rump, wasn't around a whole lot, worked double shifts just to send you to Catholic school? Knee-socks? Nuns? Sublimated desires? But you turned out okay, huh? No problems with authority, anything like that? So how long you had your badge, Sally O'Donald?"

She still wasn't sure what to make of me, but I'd cracked her composure. "I'm not convinced that's relevant, Sir." She looked nervous. Not quite sure if she should be smiling or drawing her service revolver.

"Well, I'm a detective too—a private detective. As well as an unrepentant handicap-space parker. Have been for years—a detective, I mean. So I tend to ask a lot of questions. And after you've been on the job a while I suspect you'll be a bit easier on hard-core criminal-parking types like me."

"Well, the law is the law, Sir."

"That it is, Sally. But what if—I'm speaking hypothetically of course—what if I were to drive my car away before that tow truck driver gets here?"

"A warrant could be issued, Sir. As I explained, officially your vehicle has already been impounded."

"Sally O'Donald," I said. "You're fucking me over. But in a very nice way so that maybe I ought to like it—your childish stance on life—except that it turns my stomach and reminds me of kiddie porn."

"A school teacher was sexually assaulted and killed in this parking garage," she said sternly. "We're tightening our security net."

"Yeah, I said, "I read the morning paper. Some unlucky lady gets her tits sliced and diced, so today you're out here making handicapped spaces safe for democracy."

She simply let that go and turned to leave.

"So Sally," I said. "What you doing tonight after traffic duty? Find much use for those handcuffs?"

She paused and turned, and put one hand on her gun. For the first time she almost smiled. "Frankly, Sir, I prefer the company of intelligent, sensitive women."

"Yeah," I said. "So do I. But good luck finding one who won't want to chat after her orgasm. You have a nice day."

What she gave me wasn't a smile.

CHAPTER 6

Once sensitive Officer Sally had made her semi-dramatic exit, squealing away in her cop car with the radio squawking, I didn't wait for the tow. What sensitive Sally didn't and couldn't possibly know was that I had a buddy named Glen Burgess who managed the Bridgewater impoundment garage, and I knew I could avoid complications and probably his dispatch fee by giving him a call.

Glen Burgess was a kind of institution around Bridgewater, a native son who'd come home wounded from the war in Iraq to earn a splendid living thereafter as a prodigal public servant. He'd once been a high-school athlete but had run to fat when his war wounds left him wearing a purple day-glow eye-patch and stomping around the downtown bars on a titanium leg.

Glen Burgess had a nasty habit of tearing stereos and CD players out of cars he impounded, and of reselling such equipment to supplement his already lucrative towing business. I'd occasionally sent him stereo customers myself, budget-minded audiophiles with tastes he could pander to. People, as they say, needed people, although I also secretly hated that greedy one-legged, one-eyed bastard—ambivalent, or so Lorrie would say—because Glen Burgess symbolized some grasping part of myself I didn't especially like.

But now I was at loose ends. In the past twenty-four hours I'd traveled so far across some imaginary ethical line that I had to squint to see it when I looked back. I decided it was also probably time to call up Lorrie's Mrs. Mclean simply because this was the only thing left on my list and seemed potentially profitable. One theory was, that if you kept on doing the uncomfortable things you needed to get done, sooner or later you'd have to die and that would settle that. Maybe my real problem was that my must-do/to-do list was getting kind of short lately. My thinking had turned morbid.

I headed back to my office cube where I drank a piss-warm Coors I'd stashed in my desk drawer and called Lorrie's apartment, hoping to reach her before she left for the day and getting her machine instead. I figured she'd gotten tired of waiting. So then I called Glen and got some asshole assistant who said Glen was all tied up and couldn't come to the phone. I told him I didn't want to know the kinky details but waited for him to find a pencil before I gave him my name and a complicated message about my parking ticket which I made him read back to me. Finally, after I'd postponed it as long as I could, I called Mrs. McLean—because Lorrie had given me the number after all—and I made an appointment to see her at ten o'clock Monday morning—which gave me the weekend to work myself up to it.

Then I hung up, flicked the switch on my answering-fax machine, and sat there. I was fresh out of things to do.

CHAPTER 7

So I took myself fishing—a benign way of wasting an entire autumn afternoon. Unless, of course, you happened to be an innocent fish with a sharp hook in your gullet. Fishing was something I did maybe once or twice a year, and it always felt a little out of character, but if I had hung around the office I probably would have gotten stupid drunk, which was behavior that had become so habitual of late that decided to break the pattern. I drove out to Saugamore reservoir to try my luck with an ultra-light spinning rod.

The land around the reservoir was all posted watershed: no hunting, fishing, or trespassing allowed. But since nobody was ever around to see what I was doing, I figured I'd never be noticed, and so far I'd been right.

I didn't fish in the reservoir exactly, mostly because I'd never caught anything there despite long hours of trying. Instead I preferred to wade the wide, nearly dry, boulder-strewn stream in the canyon below the dam that created the reservoir. So far as I knew, I was the only angler alive who'd ever wet a line there. It was hard work to get down and around those boulders without breaking a limb—so I claimed the privilege of the stream as the self-elected representative of all un-landed citizens, un-cliented detectives, and broken-hearted boyfriends who didn't much care if they caught anything or not.

Besides, it wasn't exactly an Ernest Hemingway kind of steam. In summer there was hardly any water at all—only an inch or so of steady flow that was whatever seeped over or through the dam— although the water level did get a boost once a week when they flushed the emergency overflow. The stream was deepest in the winter, when the flow over the dam's spillway was a gushing torrent that never froze solid. But the water was icy cold then, and dangerous and impossible to wade. Late spring and fall were best, and September just about perfect.

Today, for example. It might look to a casual observer standing on the dam that there was only two or three inches of water flowing— a trickle in which tadpoles and dusky salamanders could live, but not anything you'd want to hook. Yet somehow that was enough. There were pools—if one knew where to look for them— pockets between boulders where the water deepened to a foot or two or even three. And in these pools were fish. Sunfish mostly, and bluegills, but also a few stunted small-mouth bass. And since it basically flowed out of the reservoir, this was probably the only stream in Southern Connecticut that hadn't been trashed with rusty shopping carts pushed off highway overpasses and laced with industrial chemicals and sewer-water runoff.

You could even eat the tiny fish you caught if you were hungry and so disposed—which I wasn't. Not only was I a catch-and-release fisherman but more often than not I used barbless hooks so I wouldn't rip their little mouths. Lorrie couldn't understand the motivation—to catch something only to release it. I'd once told her it was sort of like sculpting in ice or temporarily draping the landscape with fabric. Sort of a Zen thing, a letting go. But Lorrie didn't buy my explanations. The one time I'd tried to take her fishing with me, hoping to show her a bend on this little stream that I thought of as holy ground, (and frankly daydreaming of screwing her in the open air, a splendor in the grass excursion), Lorrie never could quite get past the fact that we were trespassing on property that didn't belong to us. She explained that she saw the act of fishing on posted land not only as a act of ineffectual rebellion against authority but also as a kind of sadistic gestalt where-in I was torturing fish with my pole as a pathetic and rather transparent attempt to assert a phallocentric dominance over the natural and symbolically feminine realm. "Very astute analysis," I'd told her. "That's exactly what I'm doing."

A lot of the time I didn't bother to fish at all but simply sat around on or leaned between the boulders, meditating peacefully. It felt good to be standing in clean water and sheltered from the autumn wind. It felt good to be protected by sun-warmed rocks that caught and held the last of the season's sun. Dappled leaves would hit the surface, and I'd watch them swirl in the current, get stuck, get loose, drift on, sink and rise again a little further downstream. But Lorrie didn't understand that kind of do-nothing behavior either, didn't understand that there was more to me than the embittered shithead I appeared to be. Even psychological insight was generally something that Lorrie expected to be paid for, something important to be sandwiched neatly between appointment times. It wasn't that Lorrie wasn't a spiritual person—she was open to the possibilities of crystal jewelry and pyramid power and all manner of stupid, new-age shit. But her kind of spirituality was more of the pay-at-the-gate variety— although of course I wasn't being fair. I loved the woman and she didn't love me—or didn't love me enough, which amounted to the same thing.

CHAPTER 8

I was dog tired when I got home. I'd had to drag my weary, overweight white ass up three dark flights of wooden stairs, all the time thinking I'd had a pretty good day, having done what I'd wanted to do. I'd caught some tiny bluegills, let them go, fallen in a couple of times, gotten soaked to the knees, dried out, waded around, worn out my legs which weren't what they once had been, and reemerged with my masculine dignity—such as it was—dampened but intact.

I was so ready for a cold six-pack and a hot shower that I didn't even notice that lights were on in my apartment until I had the stairs climbed and was standing on the final landing with my graphite rod in hand. I found my door key, opened my apartment, and found myself ringed by a six-man swat-team, all of them wearing bulletproof vests and helmets. They were pointing shotguns and automatic pistols at my chest and forehead.

"Shit," I said, and slowly raised my hands.

"Down on the floor!"

I looked at my linoleum; it needed sweeping.

"Down on the floor!"

"Okay, okay," I said, and down I went. "I got bad knees." I pushed my graphite rod to one side where hopefully it wouldn't get stepped on and broken.

"Hands behind your back!"

"Jesus!"

"Hands behind your back!"

I put my hands behind my back and one guy put a pistol to my temple and stomped on my neck while another kicked me in the ass and pulled a pair of flexible plastic handcuffs tight enough to hurt my wrists.

"Easy does it," I said. "What's the problem?"

"On your feet."

"Up and down, down and up—some say ambivalence is worse than death."

For simply uttering that semi-cryptic remark another one of the swat team guys kicked me in the ribs with his boot, and it hurt so much I figured that he'd had martial arts training or else some other experience inflicting pain. I struggled to my knees. I had a cop on either side of me yanking on my arms.

"You'll notice that I'm actually being rather cooperative," I said.

"Up against the wall and spread your legs."

"Didn't that album go platinum in '69?" I asked, but I did exactly as I was told.

"And look what else I found," one of the swat team guys said. He wandered in from my bedroom carrying the single, thin-stemmed, scrawny-looking marijuana plant I'd grown from seed on my windowsill in a jelly jar that had once held an African violet. It had died on me from overwatering. "Production of a controlled substance with intent to distribute," he said. I watched him yank the plant out of the jelly jar and drop it, roots and all, into a transparent plastic evidence bag.

All this was happening as if in slow motion and felt as if it were happening to somebody else. I could feel myself being patted down, cop hands running up and down my thighs.

I heard the squawk of electronic gear and the high-pitched squeal of feedback. A voice said, "Suspect is in custody."

"10-4. Wagon's downstairs when you're ready."

I worked hard to sound reasonable. "Mind if I ask you guys a very polite question?"

"Ask away," one of the helmets said.

"Just what the fuck do you think I've done?"

"You left evidence at a murder scene. And a neighbor gave us a plate number off your car. Said your car was burning oil and looked suspicious. We got an identical plate number from an officer working traffic duty at a very similar crime scene."

I took all that in and didn't say anything at first, trying to figure what evidence I might have left, but then, because my silence did seem pretty damning, I said, "Well, maybe you want to wait for my trial before you lynch me. I'm a private detective."

"This ain't like on TV," he said, and steered me toward the stairs. I stumbled going down the staircase and the cops caught me by the armpits again and dragged me down to their car.

CHAPTER 9

I got lucky. At the police station, the swat team cleaned up its act and got semi-legal about things. Nevertheless, they locked me up alone in a six-by-six cell for nearly fourteen hours—one of those new stainless-steel holding pens with a metal bunk and a one-piece seat-less commode and drinking fountain unit and a one-way mirrored hatch in the door so they could watch me take a dump if they were so inclined. After my initial treatment I kept waiting all night for them to come and get me, half expecting to be hauled out kicking and screaming for interrogation with rubber hoses and bright lights, but they didn't. Except for providing a soggy tuna-fish sandwich on white bread sometime around midnight, the cops left me alone. There wasn't quite enough room to stretch out and sleep comfortably, and the bunk felt a little cool, but I leaned against the wall and made the best of it. If they thought solitary confinement would soften me up, they hadn't counted on the fact that I'd spent most of my adult life talking to and sometimes answering myself.

Finally, late the next morning after many hours of kidney pain and existential do-nothingness a gray-faced bailiff unlocked the cell and handcuffed me again, with my hands joined in front this time, and asked politely and calmly if I would follow him please. I decided I would do that. He led me to a small interrogation room where I sat down in a low-slung molded-plastic chair anchored with bolts to a wood floor in front of a steel desk. Then he nodded and left me to my fate.

Behind the desk sat a cop I'd casually known for years, Detective Johnny Marr—Big John, they called him—a tall, wavy-haired, middle-aged guy with the oversized neck and barrel chest of someone who'd once played semi-professional football and lifted barbells for fun. Big John probably needed his white-on-white shirts custom made. A dull gold tack held his red power tie in place. His ice-blue eyes had wrinkles at the corners that made Big John look kind of friendly until you noticed there wasn't any expression at all in them. He had a Styrofoam cup of black coffee on the desk in front of him. An unlit briar pipe rested between the carefully manicured fingertips of his large pale hands. Big John wasn't originally from Bridgewater. He'd wandered northward years ago from some tobacco town in the Carolinas, and he still had a hint of the Southern plantation in his speech and manners, so that at first you thought he was slow on the uptake, but John Marr probably had a better grade of gray matter inside his skull than most of Bridgewater's cops. He was by the book and polished, an anal type, but so far as I'd heard, he wasn't especially corrupt or cruel.

Another cop who I didn't know at all was sitting on the right-hand corner of Marr's desk and kind of sprawled across it. He was a young, rangy, brown-skinned man with full pink lips and dark Brillo-pad hair. He wore bright white tennis shoes and a wrinkled green suit with shiny pink pinstripes. It looked like the jacket and pants had been purchased separately in the kind of discount department store where they let you mix the sizes and weren't concerned about dye-lots. He didn't look like much of anything about him matched exactly. He looked to me like a middle-class black kid trying his best to look like an undercover cop pretending to be a junkie.

"Coffee?" Marr asked politely.

"Double cream, extra sugar."

Marr nodded at the young rangy man who got up and left the room briefly and brought me back a steaming cup. Marr just sat there staring at me and I stared back.

"Ain't no sugar," the rangy man said, as he handed the cup to me.

I nodded again and took it in both hands because I was still wearing the handcuffs.

"This is my new assistant, Detective Ali," Marr said.

"As our suspect, you got a right to keep silent and a right to have your attorney present during questioning. You understand?" Detective Ali asked.

I nodded and watched his eyes swing to a corner of the ceiling where the fisheye of a video camera stared down at the three of us.

"Suspect indicates by nodding that he understands his rights," I said. "Suspect suspects his rights may have already been violated."

"Disassociative response pattern," Detective Ali said. "Typical socio-pathological profile."

I glared at him and turned to Marr. "Suspect is already bored stupid by the boy-wonder detective with the college vocabulary. Suspect wants to make a phone call."

The look on Ali's face was suddenly one of twisted, barely controlled rage. I had to bite my tongue to keep from telling him I could dig it.

"That'll do, for now, Ali," Marr said. The rangy man grunted and got up and left the room again. This time he didn't come back.

"What's your problem, Lombardo?"

I shrugged.

"You were pretty hard on my young assistant. He was just showing off. He earned his master's degree in Criminology last month."

"I'm tired and sore. Your swat team got a little brutal with me last night."

"Be careful with that word *brutal*. You don't want to call my people *brutal* if you can help it."

"Speaking of calls, I understand you got an anonymous tip about a dead body," I said.

Detective Marr tapped his pipe against his palm but didn't make any attempt to light it. "Is that so?"

"That tip was from me," I said. "I made the phone call and you got it recorded—I can give it to you word-for-word."

Big John shook his head and scowled at me like scowling was something he'd learned to do so as to respond in a way that made people think he was normal. "Which tells me what exactly?"

"Exactly nothing. Only that I reported a dead body."

"We have your partial thumbprint. And a gang of teenage informants can link you to a crime scene. They tell me your Escort smokes."

"It needs rings. How'd you run my prints so fast?"

"A federal grant got us computerized. You're bonded as a private detective. Plus you've been arrested recently for DUI."

"DUI—big deal. The body was already rotten. I found a corpse and reported it. I didn't especially want to get involved. I guess you can figure why."

"Exactly what were you doing in that house?"

I sighed. "Looking for a commercial listing."

"A what?"

"Real estate," I said. "I moonlight on the side. I don't have my sales license yet. Most of the time I just take photographs of houses, but I do get around some—so to speak."

"Don't fuck with me, Lombardo."

"Check my wallet. I got some bone-colored business cards. Realty-World East and Associates. Give Jerry East a call if you don't believe me."

Marr was quiet for a moment, then he tapped his briarwood pipe against his palm again. It left a tiny ring of soot, and he pretended to study it. "Real estate, huh? Well, well, well. Making any money at it?"

"Some guys do all right."

"My son-in-law has a duplex in that neighborhood he's been trying to unload."

"Shit, have him give Jerry East a call. Just do me a favor and mention my name."

Marr's face suddenly went hard, and he slapped his palm on his desk. "What about Bill Greenwood?"

I stared at him as if I didn't understand. You could never tell about Big John. His emotional reactions were so damn phony they were real. I tried to get into the swing of things, to make myself look like I was faking looking innocent. But that was way too complicated. I gave up on faking looking innocent and simply tried playing dumb—that was easier. "Who?"

Marr looked at some papers on his desk. "Dr. William Greenwood. The deceased. The murdered guy. That faceless, prickless body on the floor—murdered and mutilated. A gynecologist by trade—except last year he'd had his license revoked—not the easiest thing to lose if you know how the A.M.A works. Seems our Dr. Greenwood liked to diddle his lady patients."

"Well," I said, "At least you won't be hard pressed to find yourself a motive. Probably lots of people hated his fucking guts."

"How about Diedre?"

"Diedre who?"

Big John reached over his desk to rub my soon-to-be bald spot with his large white knuckles. "Knock-knock. Dead Deidre with the nippleless knockers."

"You're a very funny guy, Big John."

"And how about Sue?"

"You want to give me a hint?"

"So far, a name on a note. We found your thumbprint on a pushpin holding her note to a wall. We suspect there was some cash involved."

I slapped my forehead with my manacled wrists, laying it on thick. "You know, there was this scrap of paper just lying on the stairs, and a large plastic pushpin that looked like it had fallen out. I almost stepped on it, so I picked it up. I was probably being tidy."

"This was after you discovered the body?"

"I suppose."

He jumped all over that. "You suppose? You got a dead body on the floor and you're being tidy. You're a private investigator. I can charge you with withholding evidence and impeding a murder investigation. Felony obstruction charges in addition to everything else. You know better than to contaminate a homicide scene."

"Technically it wasn't a scene yet. Nobody had reported it. I figured the guy had a heart attack and rats got to him."

"What about those nipples in that valise?"

"So far as I know it's not against any law to notice severed nipples."

Marr shook his head and dropped his volume a notch. "You know, Lombardo. You used some very profane language in the presence of one of my female traffic control officers yesterday. And you frightened her a little by talking about sex crimes. Her testimony can place you at another, very similar, homicide scene."

"No shit. I called the cops from a pay phone at the Bridgewater Shopping Plaza. I used the mall parking garage the day after they found that school-teacher's body. The story was in the paper. I even told Officer Sally as much."

"I look after my people, Lombardo. I knew this particular female officer's father."

"Shit, Big John, you know I'm not some psycho."

Marr considered this. "Get the fuck out of my office." He pressed a button on his desk and the gray-faced jailer came back to get me.

Where Ali had disappeared to, I didn't know. But on the way back to my cell I finally got to make my phone call. Lorrie answered at her apartment after the second ring, and I was damn glad to reach her.

I asked her to contact Elmo Slade, a bail bondsman I'd used before, and to drop by and see my father—the only one I knew who would lend me unsecured money—and to borrow Slade's fee from him so I could make bail.

She said she would.

CHAPTER *10*

At first, they didn't mention any murder charges at my arraignment, probably because they'd had a medical examiner look at that well-rotted corpse and realized the time of death didn't match the time they could put me at the crime scene. In fact, they didn't have any reason to hold me. The drug-production-with-intent-to-distribute charge was a felony in Connecticut, but that was a charge which would certainly be thrown out and replaced with pos-session-of-under-an-ounce-of-a-controlled-substance charge—only a misdemeanor.

But then, finally, when I was all but sure I was about to walk on my own recognizance, and had even congratulated my public defender for doing absolutely nothing to fuck things up, Marr stepped by the courtroom to explain quietly to the judge that I'd been stonewalling the cops about a murder investigation, and the magistrate upheld the distribution charge and set my bond at twenty thousand, which was the limit Elmo Slade would readily post, and released me into Lorrie's custody.

Lorrie had, of course, already met with my father to get the money and had contacted Slade as I'd asked. I knew Slade pretty well from all the times I'd been arrested for drunken driving, and for two thousand up front, he posted the twenty thousand, and sprang my poor-risk ass.

Needless to say, I was pissed, and I told Lorrie as much. By then they had obviously told her about the suitcase full of nipples. Yet she didn't even ask me any questions while driving me back home—which I figured was a bad sign—although in fairness she'd spent hours working out the details of my release and bail with Slade. I could tell she was tired and almost beyond caring. When she dropped me off at my Wood Avenue apartment she'd turned away when I bent to kiss her cheek and said, "We'll talk tomorrow, Peter.

The sky was already darkening again, night was near, and when I slammed the car door and watched Lorrie drive away, I had the terrible feeling that it was really the end of our relationship. I climbed the stairs to my apartment, unlocked the door and immediately flopped into bed, thinking that after nearly twenty-four hours without sleep I'd find oblivion and dreams at least as interesting as the ones I'd had the day before yesterday. Instead, I tossed and turned until dawn, unable to really rest, listening to the night sounds of Bridgewater—sirens and car alarms, sounds that seemed to fade away only as the sun finally rose high enough to redden the sky beyond my mini-blinds. Finally, I got up and ran tap water into a mug for instant coffee.

My apartment was an illegally zoned studio in an attic without a fire escape in a three-family tenement house on Wood Avenue that my father owned and rented out. Whenever I didn't have any place better to go I went there, but it was really only a place to store left over pizza in the rusty avocado-colored refrigerator and lie alone on a cotton futon and stack paperback books on my concrete-block-and-pine-board bookshelves. I'd lived there for nine years and it still didn't feel like home.

I had found myself a real mystery. But with no client but myself and an unsolved crime for sure, stealing a lousy two hundred dollars had already cost me big money that I'd need to pay back somehow. I couldn't afford to indulge in unsolved mysteries for long. I stood my fishing rod from last night in a grimy corner, and I tried drinking a glass of cold, thick, chocolate-flavored Instant Breakfast while I waited for the water in my mug to boil in my microwave. I almost gagged. I poured the Instant Breakfast down the drain. I found four semi-frozen strawberry Pop Tarts in my freezer compartment and put these on a paper plate and zapped them in the microwave until the sugar frosting melted. Then I sat down at the table again and drank the coffee before I went back to the refrigerator for a cold beer—I had two left.

Sam Adams Ale and instant coffee with micro-waved strawberry Pop Tarts might not be everyone's idea of a balanced breakfast, but it suited my mood. Only two days ago the idea of not having a stable identity was in the headlines of my inner life, then the idea of losing Lorrie had moved suddenly above the fold, and now the idea that I could be convicted of a felony and be so utterly without assets that I could actually be sent to prison was clamoring for my attention.

I got up from the table and walked to the toilet and took a long morning piss. "Fuck it," I said aloud. Obviously not everybody went though these kinds of upheavals—or if they did, did so with less fanfare. Obviously some people lived far worse lives. War, starvation, disease—these were problems that deserved real sympathy. A guy walking around with a designer beer and a bowl of melted sugar at six o'clock on a Monday morning wasn't exactly a candidate for anybody's pity.

I walked back into my bedroom and fiddled with my AM-FM radio. The local AM DJs were already reminding their listeners to drive safely and take the meat out of the freezer before they left for their jobs at the helicopter plant, and screaming radio preachers were hustling for contributions in the name of Jesus. On FM there was the oom-pa-pa of polkas on the Polish hour, and the weather report—cloudy...the air quality unacceptable, and some alternative jazz from the college station—the signal faint and far away.

I spent a good ten minutes in a stupor before I decided to visit my father. I had my appointment with Mrs. McLean later, and it was obviously too early to call on anybody else. Besides, I wanted to thank him for the bondsman's fee, and I knew for certain he'd be up bright and early. Before he retired at age fifty, had a coronary a year later and more or less recovered with what he liked to call "willpower," my father had risen before dawn every morning of his life. For thirty years he had worked as a supply sergeant in the U.S.

Army, and for twenty-five of those years was stationed right here in Bridgewater, where he'd worked as the army's one-man liaison with the overhaul and repair division of Bridgewater Helicopter.

A strange solitary outpost, especially for an Italian American NCO with a boot-camp-inspired value system and a slight Southern accent (the legacy of his own military-brat boyhood spent mainly in Georgia and South Florida) and no real home anywhere. No family left either—except for me and his retarded older sister, Rose, who he never visited or talked about, stashed away in a state institution somewhere on the Gulf Coast.

I believe Dad had initially thought of Bridgewater as a trading post assignment—in a remote northern region where the locals were unfriendly. But then he'd married my mother, and I'd actually been born here—not necessarily in that order—so I suspect he grew to like the place enough to put down roots. Still, all the while I was growing up, he cautioned against the dangers of going native—by which I suppose he meant failure to starch and press one's uniform. Nevertheless, he'd stayed; in fact, he'd chosen to retire in Bridgewater, and I suspect he'd secretly liked the fact that for twenty-five years in the military he'd seldom had contact with a higher ranking officer—except for the young helicopter pilots who flew choppers in and out.

His job had been a thankless one—with endless carbon forms and budget reports and complex paperwork. And for all those years he'd probably earned far less than a civilian flight mechanic, so his pension wasn't large. Still, he'd taken his duties seriously, and the rash of helicopter accidents and rotor-head failures that began in the late nineteen-nineties were probably related to the fact that he'd finally retired and wasn't around to ride herd on lackadaisical maintenance crews and make certain that paperwork repairs matched solid physical facts.

All that was behind him. After retiring from the Army, he took to managing a few rental properties he'd acquired over the years and began traveling by bus to Atlantic City to play the dollar slots with the North-End Senior Citizens. All in all, he was pretty well set. Besides his military pension and the income from the rental houses—

the three-family on Wood Avenue where I had my attic apartment now, and a duplex on George Street, where we'd lived when I was a little kid—he owned and occupied a big red-brick split-level up by the county line. The house had a faulty security system—for which I was held responsible because the last time I'd gotten desperate enough to try commissioned sales I'd sold him an overpriced motion detector that didn't work very well and tried to make it up to him by installing the thing for free. Ordinarily, I didn't feel sorry for my father. He'd bought twelve acres and the house for thirty-grand in 1969, paid off a no-money down VA mortgage over the next thirty years, and watched real estate prices in suburban Connecticut rise so quickly in the interim that somewhere along the way he got richer than Midas and started thinking of himself as a savvy investor.

I used the key under the black rubber mat to let myself in. I came upon him sitting in a leatherette Lazyboy in his yellow wallpapered living room, watching TV, eating unsalted peanuts by the handful, and washing them down with slugs of instant Sanka—a dietary combination he thought of as health food.

"I wanted to thank you for the bail money, Pop."

He glanced at me and shook his head. He'd lost most of his hair to male-pattern baldness and was always after me to cut my own hair short and shave. The few thin strands he had left were combed carefully across his crown. "You look like shit," he said. "When you going to get a real job and marry that little colored girl?"

The "little colored girl" was Lorrie, of course, and I had already tried explaining any number of times that I already had a real job. I worked—albeit irregularly—as a private detective. I'd also explained that Lorrie was philosophically opposed to marriage on the grounds that it was demeaning to women and a form of sexual enslavement and that basically I agreed with her about all that. Besides, I had already twice asked her to marry me, and both times she'd said no.

He looked at me and sighed again and used the remote to kick on his VCR. He'd videotaped old episodes of The People's Court. Judge Wapner was deciding on a complicated case; a terminal AIDS patient had pummeled a Bible salesman. I didn't stay to see how it turned out. "Use your head out here," my father said. "Don't take stupid chances."

I deadbolted his door behind me.

CHAPTER *11*

"Out there" was Bridgewater—the armpit of Southern Connecticut—a mid-sized factory town that had fallen on hard times. Bridgewater was what the media people meant when they spoke of the rust belt. Empty steel mills, deserted foundries, bankrupt tool works and munitions plants, entire factories gone dark and rusty or else moved—one after another—either to Mexico or China, where labor and bribes were cheaper. The unemployment rate in Bridgewater had hovered for decades at nearly twenty percent—higher for blacks and Hispanics. Domestic violence was rampant, alcohol and drug abuse widespread, robberies so common that the Bridgewater Telegram no longer bothered to report such crimes, and homicides were at an all-time high. It was a good place to be a private investigator if you didn't mind bribing bureaucrats to keep your business license.

Bridgewater hadn't had an honest city official in nearly five decades. And even back then it had probably been a fluke. A strong blue-collar turnout had elected a Socialist mayor, Jasper McLean, in 1932 and kept on re-electing him by landslides until November 1958 when the remaining vestiges of red-scare McCarthyism had finally provoked sufficient fear in the local electorate to put a party-machine Republican in office and drive old Mayor McLean to an auto-exhaust-fume suicide in his own detached garage.

In the early 1960s, the city's new administration immediately sold off half the town's parkland so as to re-route Interstate 95, which was being planned back then. Such re-routing was deemed necessary for locating exit ramps and feeders. All this "urban renewal" had inevitably required the acquisition of tenement housing owned by party officials who sold property to the government at enormously inflated prices. Not only did the deal create a sudden dearth of affordable low-income rentals, but it had subsequently required the city to embark on massive low-income housing construction projects with appropriate kickbacks from corrupt contractors.

It took only a few short years before those solid Republicans had looted the city's diminished tax-base of the point of fiscal ruin, and the citizens finally got wise, so the Democrats made peace with those same suspect contractors, bought the election wholesale, and took their turn at the trough. Most recently, the city had been governed by a succession of "fiscally conservative" Democratic lawmakers who kept getting indicted by a federal task force for racketeering and extortion but nevertheless got re-elected by promising to do something about crime.

Bridgewater's current mayor, the Honorable Hiram "High Hopes" Silverstone, was yet another rotten apple in a very mushy barrel. His most recent popular "cause" was the property rights of land owners. These "rights," so far as I could determine, had something to do with the readiness of his financial supporters to bury hazardous waste, mostly incinerated ash from the Federal Superfund sites, on privately-owned land with the city's corporate limits.

While Mayor Silverstone was supposedly "personally uncomfortable" with such toxic waste burial "for "ecological reasons," he was willing to pay big bucks from the city's nearly empty tax coffers to compensate supportive landowners for the loss of potential revenue—dumping fees from the as-yet entirely imaginary private landfills that the city's preemptively restrictive zoning laws had supposedly prohibited them from operating.

Also, as recently as last winter, I'd heard rumors that about half the Bridgewater city council was once again being investigated by the Feds for having deliberately hired a twice-convicted arsonist to provide on-site security for the town's abandoned train station—probably in an effort to collect on the fire insurance policy as well as to make a lucrative post-inferno demolition contract available for awarding to well-connected friends.

An entire homeless family—a mom, a dad, and a couple of infant girls—had been fried to an unrecognizable crisp in the resulting conflagration. For a week or two, there had been whispers around town that this time they'd simply gone too far, that there were, after all, some limits. But after another week or so, the rumors ceased—or else turned to jokes about the big Bridgewater barbecue. A city coroner still had the charbroiled remains of the family on ice for evidence if the ongoing investigation ever came to anything, but nothing ever came to anything in Bridgewater.

Socialist or not, old Mayor McLean was still spoken of with respect and nostalgic fondness by geriatric retirees even older than my father as the man who had refused to plow the streets during the blizzard of 1935 on the grounds that the "Good Lord put the snow there and the good Lord would take it away."

I wasn't sure that kind of unsophisticated political message would fly quite as well these days, but back in the nineteen thirties only the well-to-do owned cars, and a city still trying to weather the Great Depression couldn't afford to pay its snowplow drivers overtime. But so far as anyone knew, Jasper McLean had never stolen a dime from anyone, had never laid off a city employee, and had never raised property taxes in his twenty-eight years in office. The worst thing anyone could say about him was that—during his final term, not long before his last hurrah—the randy old dog had acquired a trophy wife, a woman thirty years his junior, but that perk of power wasn't exactly uncommon—then or now. Hell, a lot of sexy young women were attracted to older men—or at least I hoped they were.

McLean's widow still lived on the south side of town, in a huge decaying Victorian house with a one-acre rose garden surrounded by the aging campus of the University of Bridgewater, a fully-accredited private college that had seen far better days. In fact, a controlling majority presence on the board of trustees had been acquired a few years back by a group called Islamic Brightness—a fundamentalist cult so far as I could tell—which, in a supposedly fortuitous turn of events, had saved the institution from fiscal insolvency.

The University, like the city, had been about to go belly up, but a thirty-five-million-dollar donation—wired via Switzerland from the United Arab Emirates—had turned the financial tide.

But long before those Islamist trustees had purchased the right to award fully-accredited baccalaureate degrees to hard-core true believers, Jasper McLean had been one of the institution's original co-founders, and although at the time of his suicidal demise his house had been willed entirely to the University—ostensibly to endow a scholarship for needy students, there was also an extensive codicil to the bequest that gave his widow the right to continue to occupy their home until she too had gone, gently or not, into that good night.

Mrs. Mclean had never remarried and had lived there ever since. She'd absolutely refused to vacate her property for fear that the Islamic folk would order her rose garden bulldozed and demolish her ornate old house to construct some huge energy-efficient indoctrination hall on the site, which was exactly what they'd done with most of the other gingerbread Victorians that the University had once owned.

I'd learned most of this dirt from Jerry East, who, like every other real-estate hustler in Bridgewater had approached Jasper McLean's widow at one time or another, hoping to broker a sweetheart deal and pocket a big commission, but she'd turned them all away. "I enjoy being surrounded by young people," she'd told him. "The University will have to wait." I mistrusted this explanation because of its simplicity, but it endeared Mrs. McLean to me for reasons I barely understood. I'd had my own difficulties with the University in the short time I'd been a student there—long before the Islamic Brightness folk took over. I was attracted to evidence of stubbornness, I think, a kink I'd have to ask Lorrie to probe.

I wondered if I might still qualify as a young man in Mrs. McLean's eyes. I was rapidly approaching my forty-seventh birthday; I was thirty pounds overweight; I had salt and pepper hair, and I was already begun to go bald like my father. And although wide brim fedoras and trench coats with big shoulder epaulets weren't the way private detectives had ever dressed, except maybe in the movies, my costume looked good and felt right. I figured it might impress a potential client. Anyway, that was what I was wearing as I slammed the car door on my dangling trench-coat belt. I reopened the door and slammed it again, cursed, and looked around to see if anybody was watching or if there was anybody but myself I could blame for a bent buckle. I headed for the gate in the white picket fence that surrounded the McLean estate and hesitated a long moment to collect myself before I lifted the latch to head up the wet flagstone path. A cold drizzle was falling from a gray overcast sky, with the air so caustic with fumes from the city incinerators and the coal-fired smokestacks of United Illuminating that standing there with my hand on the gate looking over Mrs. McLean's rose garden I longed for a place and time of innocence I'd never possessed.

I'd become a private investigator nearly twenty nine years ago— right after the University of Bridgewater had expelled me in my sophomore year for shooting a porno film in my dorm room with the school's camera equipment and trying to peddle it to the local mob for distribution. I'd been planning to be an English major with minors in Philosophy and Communications, so I'd tried calling it an art flick, hoping to bullshit my way out of the pending expulsion, but one look at the unedited rushes and the Dean of Students had readily concluded that redeeming social value wasn't what I'd had in mind. The ironic thing was that the scene they found most objectionable, the one with the big Doberman, hadn't been my idea.

The film's canine co-star was a gentle family pet and had accompanied one of the underage coeds I'd hired. She'd brought him along as her bodyguard because she didn't feel the Bridgewater campus was particularly safe at night—which it wasn't—and decided of her own volition to give him a doggy treat so sordid that one look at the work print would have given Dr. Freud bad dreams. The girl's parents had been irate. So somebody had to take the fall, and I'd been the eye behind the camera. Needless to say, my old man hadn't been pleased, and the poor Doberman involved had been gassed at the city pound.

Anyway, that was college, and I'd never gone back. I made my way up some sagging wood stairs that needed paint to a big white front porch where I found myself staring at a gargoyle hound-of-hell doorknocker that wouldn't lift off the door. It took me a minute to realize the knocker was lacquered in place and to find the electric doorbell.

I stood there long enough to start wondering if anybody was at home before Mrs. McLean answered the chimes. Then she opened the door a crack and stared at me from behind the bronze security chain. She was a tiny wrinkled woman—no more than five feet tall, with wide, pale blue eyes and a confused expression on her face. Her hair was white and wispy, and as she fingered the chain I could see she was leaning on a thick ivory walking stick carved with an intricate totem-pole design that looked like something Captain Ahab had jabbed at Moby Dick. There was obviously some kind of nasty karma at work. Just last week Lorrie had insisted that I pledge five dollars to Save the Whales.

"Mrs. McLean?" I said. "I'm Pete Lombardo." I looked at my watch—a Rolex case with ten dollar guts. 10:00—I was right on the money. "We had an appointment?"

"Mr. Lombardo," she said, and unfastened the door, and led the way inside. I followed the click of her cane through a small dim foyer and into a small sitting room with dusty accordion blinds, red Egyptian carpets, a flowered green-velvet loveseat with dark oak arms, a coffee table, and a straight-backed chair with an embroidered seat. Collapsible plastic trays flanked it on each side. There was some amateurish knitting on one of the trays. Against one wall, an old console-style television with a dusty screen had been topped with a lace doily that protected it from rabbit-ears augmented with aluminum foil.

"Do sit down," she said.

I sat down on the velvet loveseat so that she could have the straight-back chair and unbelted my coat and put my wet hat on my lap. The loveseat sagged, and I felt pretty awkward. The room seemed way too small. I stared up at the elaborate but dirty plaster work of her ceiling.

"Give me your hat."

I stood up again and gave her my fedora. She carried it away somewhere and when she returned she had shed the cane and was carrying an antique silver tea service that needed a good polishing. I stood up and helped her lower the heavy tray to a rosewood coffee table.

"You'll have tea?" she asked, but it wasn't really a question. She might look like a sweet old lady, but I didn't grow up a Army brat without learning something about rigid thinking. Mrs. McLean's mental processes were about as flexible as cast aluminum.

She poured two tiny porcelain cupfuls. "Cream or lemon?"

"Lemon," I said, and wiggled my pinkie at her.

"I would have guessed, lemon. Lorrie always prefers lemon, but then she's fond of the herbal teas."

I didn't say anything to that, but I could somehow imagine Lorrie sitting here, having tea with Mrs. McLean. I still wasn't sure if she was one of Lorrie's screwy friends, a grandmotherly figure with whom she exchanged intimacies, a wealthy agoraphobic patient who required frequent house-calls—or some strange combination of client and confidante. As a therapist Lorrie wasn't exactly afraid of blurring her professional and personal boundaries. Which I couldn't really complain about, seeing as how I got to sleep with her.

"She recommends you very highly, Mr. Lombardo."

I shrugged. At least Mrs. McLean looked like she could afford my fees. "So what did she tell you?"

"She tells me you're a functioning paranoid, entirely trustworthy, with absolutely no respect for authority."

I considered for a minute before I answered. I picked up a tarnished spoon and stared at my distorted face in it. "I'm not especially trustworthy," I said.

When Mrs. McLean laughed, it was the tinkling laugh of a person who'd known deep sorrow and learned to laugh at trifles. It was a musical laugh with something reserved about it, and I immediately decided I liked Mrs. McLean more than I liked most people on short acquaintance. "Your candor proves the point, Mr. Lombardo. But honesty often masks false pride just as irony masks impotence."

I shook my head. It was getting far too complicated, and I wasn't about to sit here and trade aphorisms and sing the blues. "What was it you wanted to see me about, Mrs. McLean?"

She closed her eyes and put down her tiny teacup very deliberately with both hands. It rattled as she set it down. "Murder," she said softly. "About murder, Mr. Lombardo."

This was a little too theatrical. I put down my teacup, too.

"So who do you want killed?"

She opened her pale blue eyes wide again, and although I secretly suspected she wasn't at all shocked, I felt a little guilty for what I knew I was about to do. "Nobody hires a private detective like me to investigate anything important," I said. "I mostly do divorce work. Either I find indifferent fathers who aren't paying child support, or else I take gritty photos of unfaithful wives. Murder—well, that's either official police business or else something for TV detectives. If the cops can't find a killer, an independent operative can't. People who hire real-life private investigators are looking for something different—they're usually romantics who want justice or revenge, sometimes both." I hesitated, for effect. "So who do you want killed, Mrs. McLean?"

She shook her head ever so slightly. "You have a streak of cruelty beneath your candor, Mr. Lombardo."

I sat there quietly and squeezed a lemon wedge at my tea. It was hard to stay nonchalant when I squirted my left eye—which started to tear a bit.

She studied me before she spoke. I dabbed at my eye with the edge of a napkin.

"You have heard of my late husband, Jasper? And of his so-called suicide?"

I nodded. "So-called," I said. I'd learned about the virtue of repeating things from hanging around Lorrie, and before her, from a long series of other discount shrinks.

"It was murder," said Mrs. McLean. "And I have desired revenge for over fifty years."

"Fifty is a lot of years," I said. My eye seemed mostly recovered.

"There's no statute of limitations in murder cases."

"Not legally," I said. "But the bodies eventually rot."

"Do you believe in reincarnation, Mr. Lombardo?" Her pale blue eyes were darting around with a kind of frantic eagerness.

I hesitated. I hadn't been expecting this. I needed a paying client badly, but I wasn't about to start talking trash to white-haired ladies. "Maybe in the intestines of worms," I said.

She sighed. "My late husband was a very good man, Mr. Lombardo, but unlike you he was old and so very unworldly."

"How so?" I asked. I was easily flattered but I wasn't young, and I'd never considered myself particularly worldly.

"He believed that most people are basically good hearted."

"And you don't think so?"

"Forgive me, Mr. Lombardo, but most men are basically swine."

I thought about being offended, but I'd been in a rut for the last few years, and I hadn't been able to muster much indignation about anything. Besides, philosophically speaking, I agreed with her: most men were swine, but most women were swine too. For want of something clever to say, I scratched my head and tried my best to look interested.

"A man like Jasper would never take his own life," she said.

"Why's that?"

Mrs. McLean pounded the sides of her chair with her fists like a seven-year-old girl having a tantrum.

"He simply wouldn't," she said. "I would have known if he'd been despondent."

Regret, I thought, because she'd missed the warning signs.

"Okay," I said. "So he wasn't despondent."

"And I'm quite sure he was murdered," she said.

"Quite sure?" I put the emphasis on the "quite."

"Well, our garage door was locked," she said with some finality.

I pretended to ponder this. I took up a classical posture with chin in hand. Pete Lombardo, the thinker. "Maybe he locked the garage to make sure he'd go through with dying even if he changed his mind."

"They never found the key," she said.

"Okay," I said. "Let's say he was murdered."

She nodded.

"So maybe you know who killed him?"

"Were I to know who killed him, should I not wish to employ a professional hit man rather than a private detective who rankles at the notion of being one?"

She not only had a point, but an elegant command of the subjunctive.

"Did he have any enemies?" It was a stupid question, but I felt like I had to ask it anyway. Going through the motions.

"All men in positions of power make enemies. Very few are murdered."

"When you're cold, you're cold," I said.

She frowned.

"How about sexual or romantic involvements?" I rolled my eyes, trying to make her smile.

"To the best of my knowledge he was an entirely faithful husband, and frankly I am offended by your suggestion."

"Look, Mrs. McLean. Are you absolutely sure you want me clamming in your past. Sometimes it's better to let things go."

In response, she handed me a check for thirty-five-hundred dollars. It was made out to CASH in what seemed a very shaky hand. My heartbeat began to accelerate.

I folded the check in half and quickly stuck it in my wallet. I found a notepad in my raincoat pocket and a pen in my shirt pocket, and I wrote out a receipt: "*Received from Mrs. Jasper McLean, a thirty-five-hundred dollar retainer for investigative services. Investigative fees to be two hundred fifty dollars per diem plus expenses. Client to be consulted before any single day's expenses are allowed to exceed an additional two hundred fifty dollars.*" I wrote up this crap and signed it and handed it to Mrs.

McLean who waited patiently until I was done then held up her palm and shook her head.

"Trust, Mr. Lombardo," she said. "A noble ideal, don't you agree?"

"Right again," I said, and crumpled up the receipt. "A noble ideal." All the more noble, I thought, because the check had become untraceable and I could cheat on my income tax.

"Well, I trust that you'll begin your investigations immediately," Mrs. McLean said.

"And where do you suggest I begin?"

"That, Mr. Lombardo, is entirely up to you. If I were you, I should discover a motive."

She stood up, I stood up, and she extended her delicate hand. I'd been dismissed. Neither of us had drunk our tea, and I didn't remember my fedora until I was already halfway out the door.

CHAPTER *12*

I was still south of the downtown banking district, headed north up Main Street between the concrete-block housing projects that towered above me like the walls of an eroded canyon, when the first of the bullets passed cleanly through my car. The sound was something like a burp—but much louder and more metallic. It was a nasty sound, and at first I didn't connect it with the tiny hole that seemed to materialize in my Escort's roof, showering me with a fine and no doubt carcinogenic dust, and the larger hole—about the size of a coffee can—that was suddenly *there*, in the floorboards between the seats, where black asphalt went whizzing by.

I swerved into the left-hand lane just as a second hole appeared in the roof and I heard a sharp ping as the slug clipped the plastic grip off the gear-shift knob before it too went on through.

I mashed down hard on the gas pedal and didn't let up on it until I was four or five miles away and still exceeding the speed limit by thirty miles per hour and about to pass an unmarked patrol car on the right. The cop gave me a disapproving look, so I braked and fell into line behind him. I took the next left turn—which was the entrance to the Monroe Shopping Park, a busy suburban shopping mall still known locally as Korvettes after a long-defunct department store that had anchored the mall in its earliest years. Almost casually, I coasted down to a cluster of cars by a secondary entrance. I found an empty parking space, cut the engine, and sat there for a moment shaking and cursing before I climbed out and examined the bullet holes in my roof. I even stuck my finger through and wiggled it around like a puppet. The hole was as smooth-sided as one drilled by a punch press—which meant a high velocity rifle. What bothered me was the way the slug had expanded like a bad metaphor before it found its way through the floor. I disliked guns as much as anybody, and had sense enough to fear them, but I didn't know shit about ballistics, and that kind of expansion seemed out of the ordinary. It was probably specialty ammo, something military maybe. There ought to be a law, and of course there was, although it didn't mean jack, so I locked the car doors and rolled up the windows and headed in to buy some lunch.

The Burger King inside the mall had a long line and everyone in it suddenly looked like a sociopath. A massive black woman in a purple dress was slapping her kids around. A bony-assed older gent in a polyester running suit and black FBI wing-tips kept taking furtive glances over his shoulder. A Puerto Rican guy in baggy pants stood tweaking his sparse goatee and rolling his bloodshot eyes backward until only the whites showed. I tried focusing on the electronic menu display. This was probably a safe enough place to eat. I wouldn't get food poisoning, and I needed to settle down and think clearly.

Why would someone want me dead? Good reasons for murders were always the same: sex or money or revenge or power—or some combination of those four. I couldn't for the moment think of how finding a dead body or a suitcase full of nipples might make me a target. Nor could I simply assume there was some connection between my being hired to investigate Jasper McLean's death and the immediate attempt on my life. I'd already discounted the possibility of coincidence—although how anybody could know so soon that I'd been by to see Mrs. McLean—I couldn't tell.

Still, the more I thought about those holes in my Escort, the more pissed-off I became. Behind the anger was fear, and behind the fear—more fear, but when bullets start flying, self-consciousness becomes a luxury. Some years ago, long before I'd met Lorrie, I'd once consulted a very expensive cognitive psychiatrist about my relationship with my father and a general pervasive feeling of worthlessness that had been troubling me for some time.The good doctor had listened closely for nearly an hour while I explained the ins and outs of me, and then he'd asked a single pointed question: "How much do you make a year?"When I answered him honestly, he explained that I couldn't possibly afford to deal with such problems. At the time I'd been offended—I'd never gone back, but over the years I'd come to see that he'd been right. I had yet to earn the right to indulge certain feelings—at least on a permanent basis. If I wanted to work as a private detective I had to stay in constant motion and siphon in only enough residual anger to keep me moving. If there was some connection between McLean's murder and the holes in my Escort, I could pretty much rule out sex as a motive—except, of course, as Lorrie would insist, in some broad neo-Freudian sense *everything* came down to sex. But McLean had been dead for fifty years, so it was highly unlikely we'd shared a common partner. Besides, I hadn't been unfaithful to Lorrie in at least a month, and she knew and didn't mind.

So, unless somebody had tried to cover up a sex-related carbon monoxide poisoning—which wasn't likely—money or power was the key—which certainly covered a lot of territory. McLean had been the mayor, which meant political patronage.He controlled tax revenues for a mid-sized city, which meant a budget in the millions. Fifty years ago someone had probably become rich or powerful when he'd died in that locked garage, and maybe that money or power was still up for grabs.

Since a lump sum of money would have long since been dispersed and laundered, and, as political power is by definition unstable, perhaps I was looking for a fifty-year-old political decision that had made somebody wealthy and/or powerful and/or con-tinued to do so. Either that or I was out of my mind.

I took a long deep breath, held it, and then exhaled. It had been a long time since I'd had to think very hard.There wasn't much call for thinking in the kind of detective work I did, and I was amazed to discover I could still make complex connections.My body might be that of a middle-aged fast food junkie, but my mind wasn't addled. It felt good to be exercising the gray matter in a way that didn't lead directly to self pity. But I didn't like being motivated by bullets.

The line had moved forward and I found myself staring into the freckled face of a sixteen-year-old girl with a few loose brown hairs that had escaped her uniform cap. I found her attractive and felt guilty about wanting her, and angry at myself for feeling guilty. I wasn't quite a dirty old man—not yet anyway.

"Whopper and onion rings," I said.

"Anything to drink, Sir?"

"Diet Pepsi," I said. "I'm counting calories where I can."

She smiled shyly, then turned away to fill my order.

CHAPTER *13*

To see Lorrie during her working day I had to make an appointment. She was currently employed by an organization called AIPA which was an acronym for some kind of taxpayer-supported social-service agency, and fortunately, although I was already stored deep in their computer banks as paranoid, passive-aggressive, bipolar, and alcohol dependent, and as someone struggling to control messianic impulses, I'd made it a point never to use my real name with her receptionist. Foolish as it seemed, I kept protecting my long-term options. Who knew what the future might hold? Someday I might want to go into politics. Maybe I'd run for mayor or congress or even the U.S. presidency—sweep the New Hampshire primary and start a little slush fund. I didn't want any psychological case history screwing up my chances. Besides, I wanted to see Lorrie as often as I wished and to pay the lowest possible sliding fee—five dollars a session. On the books I was indigent and chronic—which unfortunately wasn't far from true. I ordinarily wore a horsehair moustache to my therapy sessions, and although on some level I knew that I wasn't really fooling anybody, I felt a lot more comfortable in disguise.

Actually, I never minded paying five dollars a session to see Lorrie. I probably did need to see a therapist regularly—and paying the five dollars made our time together seem more valuable somehow. In fact, on the infrequent occasions when we'd made use of her office couch for probings other than our psychoanalytic ones, paying the five dollars had given me a kinky thrill I'd never mentioned to Lorrie for fear she'd explain the fun out of it. Also, she tended to be vocal in her lovemaking, and I didn't want to embarrass her. I also carefully avoided mentioning that I suspected the middle-aged receptionist in the outer office was on to us. She was always giving me snide looks, peering over her bifocals with a pale, prudish face that seemed to register disapproval every time I showed up for an appointment. Maybe. Or maybe not. It could have been my imagination.

A buzzer on the receptionist's desk sounded. I surreptitiously adjusted my mustache; she openly adjusted her wig. It was a cheap, dark wig, but somehow suited her perfectly. If you were going to wear a mask, it might as well be an ugly one.

"Ms. Moore will see you now, Mr. Khan."

I put down a magazine article about bass-fishing in Alabama and stood up. Someday I wanted to go fishing in some pristine Southern swamp—but I didn't believe I'd ever get around to doing it, and maybe that was for the best.

Lorrie stood in the hallway alongside her office, looking Woodstock-nation chic in her long, Indian-print skirt, short-sleeved blouse, and leather flats. She was a little too skinny, and today her dark hair was pulled back into a kind of frizzy braided ponytail, and she wasn't wearing any make-up on her copper-brown skin—she rarely did. There was an aura of soundness and sincerity about Lorrie that I inevitably found attractive, although I suppose she could be called mousey or even plain by someone who didn't know her. She smiled and turned, and I followed her down the industrial-carpeted hallway and into her tiny windowless office. She locked the door with a delicious click and immediately she was in my arms. A very pleasant and unexpected greeting indeed—especially after our argument last night. Her small firm breasts pressed against me. But she never wanted to kiss me when I was wearing my fake moustache.

"Mr. Khan," she said. "Baby, that thing has got to go."

"*Kubla* to my friends," I said.

Lorrie smiled. "You have absolutely no shame, Peter."

"Isn't that the point of therapy?"

"Is it?"

"You're good," I said.

"Still," she insisted, "you'll admit that Kubla Khan is a little literary."

"Literary nothing," I said. I winced as I pulled off my moustache. "I'm Bridgewater U. Alum. You questioning my street cred?"

When Lorrie laughed it was like wind-chimes on the evening veranda. There weren't many people that I could say that about. As a general rule, I mistrusted laughter. There was nearly always something cruel in it.

"I've been thinking about last night, Peter" she said, finally getting down to it.

"And?"

"I talked to Captain Marr this morning."

"The fucker."

"He says you reported a horrific crime that you didn't really have to get involved in, that your story checked out, and that they'll probably drop the pot charge."

"Then that Dudley-Do-Right motherfucker cost me two-thousand dollars for nothing."

"I'm on your side, Peter," Lorrie said, "although growing grass in your own apartment was really a very stupid move."

"I stuck a couple of seeds in a jelly jar. I had an African violet but it died on me—not enough natural light."

"You probably need to find another place to live. Surely it's not a healthy dynamic to rent an apartment from your father."

"I'm considering relocating to a crack house on the East Side," I said. "It used to be a roller-skating rink. Nowadays it's supposedly a mosque. We'll go visit the homeboys. Smoke a pipe some Saturday night."

"I'll pass," she said. Then she frowned, and I could tell she was starting to think like a psychologist. Lorrie got all hung up sometimes about being half-white and well-educated as if she were betraying some racial loyalty she had no real reason to have.

I gave her a look that was unabashedly erotic. "Indeed you will."

Lorrie had a sandglass—actually a three-minute egg timer filled with salt—that she kept on her desk. She picked it up and turned it with a flick of her delicate wrist. Tiny white grains of sea-salt began to run. Sea salt from a health-food store.

"I find it helps people get to the point," she said.

"Am I people?"

Lorrie sighed. "All too human," she said.

I turned the hourglass upside-down again.

"Let's hope your clients aren't suicidal," I said. "You certainly wouldn't want to hurry them along."

"Are we feeling self destructive today?" There was enough sarcasm in her voice to annoy me. I was already sarcastic enough for any twelve detectives, something about myself I didn't especially like—not that I was about to change.

"If you ain't suicidal, you ain't shit. One of these days I'm going to get me a bumper sticker printed."

"Are you drinking again?" She sounded concerned now.

"Not especially, I said. "I'd let you know."

Lorrie leaned forward and kissed the bridge of my nose. It was hardly worth taking off the moustache. "So what brings you to therapy, Mr. Khan."

"You mean besides wanton lust?"

She almost blushed. "Certainly," she said. "Besides that."

"I met with Mrs. McLean today."

"Really?"

"She wants me to investigate a fifty-year-old murder."

"Well?"

"I took the case."

"Well, I'm glad," Lorrie said." She needs somebody besides me who believes in her."

"I wouldn't go that far."

"But you took the case."

"I needed the money."

"To which extent do our motivations matter?" It was meant to be a rhetorical question, but that a psychoanalyst would even ask it was testimony to something.

"Live, shit, and die," I said.

"You're in an ugly mood, Mr. Khan." She was smiling still, but she hated it when I got bitter about my life.

"About an hour ago somebody put two bullets through my Escort."

Lorrie wasn't smiling now. She was silent for a moment. "Do you think there's some connection?"

"Allah only knows," I said, and smiled. "The city's rife with psychos. It could be random violence." I cocked my finger and pretended to fire six bullets into her wall.

"So you're keeping the case?" She was smiling again. I was glad she found me amusing.

"I don't like people shooting at me, and I don't like taking my car into body shops and dealing with ex-cons. Shit, it's humiliating even to own an Escort."

"A horror!" Lorrie said, then she hesitated. "The shooting, I mean."

I smiled, but something about the way she'd reacted bugged me. For all her education, compassion, and insight, Lorrie had lived a sheltered life, and the people she dealt with were, after all, the ones who, crazy or not, gave a fuck about the way they felt. Cold-blooded killers were another kind entirely and Lorrie didn't understand them at all—or anyway not as well as I did, seeing as how I sometimes had it in me to be one. Nothing in Lorrie's background had prepared her for people who engaged in deliberate violence. Her parents were mild, reasonable people. Dark skinned though she was, she'd grown up carefree as a chocolate-milk Heidi on a goat farm in upstate New York, where her mother, a vague, frail-looking woman whom I'd met once when she visited, taught high-school biology, and her father, an older black man, already five years in his grave, but gray and distinguished in a wallet-photo I'd seen, had been a professor emeritus who'd once held an endowed chair in Comparative Literature at Colgate.

"Did you by any chance tell anyone that I was going to visit Mrs. McLean?"

Lorrie hesitated a moment. "Well, I might have mentioned it in passing to Salvadore Almonde."

I slapped my own face. Twice. Hard. Using my open palm. Forehand and backhand. *Thanks, I needed that. A* theatrical gesture that felt false even as I followed through. I'd borrowed it from an old TV commercial for a once popular aftershave, but privately it was associated with a very painful memory. The slogan reminded me of Andy Burnside, an old Army buddy of my father's, a seemingly warm avuncular guy once so close enough to our family that as a kid I'd actually called him Uncle Andy—until, of course, he ran off with my mother and I never saw either of them again. Unlike my Dad, Andy Burnside had managed to leave the military behind him after serving a tour in Vietnam. He had taken a job as a copy-writer for a Manhattan ad agency. He'd come up with that aftershave slogan back when he'd been a boozer. He was dead now too, poor bastard, of liver disease. *Thanks, I needed that.* Love taps from the underbelly of my past. Lorrie didn't say anything, but she shook her head—she'd heard all about Uncle Andy.

"Sal Almonde's one step from the very top of the New York mob families," I said. "How the fuck do you know him?"

Lorrie hesitated. "Well," she said. "He's my patient."

"Here?" I looked around at her pastel walls and ferns and was aghast. In a world where crime bosses sought psychotherapy at taxpayer-supported agencies, civilization couldn't endure very long. Human beings were doomed; extinction loomed; we'd never colonize the stars—I didn't know why I felt this, but it certainly seemed true.

"Private practice," Lorrie said, and smiled. She saw a few patients on the side to supplement her agency income. Mostly older people like Mrs. McLean who still attached some stigma to seeing a shrink and had the discretionary income necessary for an extended analysis. "He's really into it," Lorrie said. "He had an abusive childhood."

"Jesus," I said. "He's a Don, for Christ's sake! And aren't you supposed to keep your client's problems confidential?"

"He's a highly intelligent seventy-six-year-old man. He's in pain. He has regrets."

"Yeah," I said. "He has regrets, two bodyguards, a mansion in

Weston, about three dozen grandchildren, a Big-Boy tomato patch, and the heroin franchise for Southern Connecticut."

"Drug-dealing's not an ethical problem in his value system," Lorrie said, and hesitated before she explained. "If you accept moral values as culturally relative, you can't simply reject those you don't happen to like."

"That must be one of those affirmative action type ideas," I said. "It needs a little mercy to hold its own in the marketplace."

Lorrie smiled. "Are you attacking me, Peter?"

"I don't want to see you hurt."

"Sal cried when he saw *The Godfather*," Lorrie said. She seemed pretty upset for some reason. "In some ways he's quite accessible. I've got him reading Sartre and Simone de Beauvoir. We're doing existential therapy."

"He'll erase your existence if you rub him wrong."

Lorrie smiled. "I can handle Sal Almonde," she said. "Don't go yielding to one of your protective macho fantasies. Besides he's entitled to feel things—like anybody."

"Wouldn't dream of interfering with treatment. But I'd rather you leave my name and Mrs. McLean's out of it."

She sighed as if I'd made her feel guilty. "I only mentioned you as someone I knew professionally, and Sal was the one who brought up Mrs. McLean. He knew her in the old days, and he likes to reminisce. During World War II, Bridgewater was quite the boom town."

"Humor me," I said. "Loose lips sink ships."

She put her arms around my neck again. "Poor baby," she said. "I can see you've had a rotten morning."

CHAPTER *14*

I got into my car and drove quickly down Main Street to Columbia. To beat the light at Lisbon Pizza, I turned right down Columbia between New York Carpet and Sorrento's Importing, then left again onto Madison at the Yurgin's Hardware intersection. I followed Madison to Earl Street and Vinny's Variety Store, where I turned left again and followed Earl back to Main and the corner where the plate glass window of the Caveat Supply Co. displayed wheelchairs and bedpans and an assortment of prosthetic limbs. I turned right on Main and took the very next right fork, traveling up the steep hill on North Jefferson Avenue where I finally got stopped by a no-turn red light I couldn't run.

I knew exactly where I was going and I wasn't looking forward to it. Salvadore Almonde kept office hours, normally by appointment only, in an apartment above his funeral home. He didn't live above the funeral home any longer or have anything much to do with the practical end of running the mortuary. It had been his father's business, and was still known locally as Almonde's—although Sal Senior, an old-time Sicilian capo, had long since availed himself of the talents of his best embalmer and moved on to smaller quarters. Nowadays, Sal's funeral parlor was run by some cousins on his mother's side, and although working for the Almonde family had occasionally required said cousins provide mortuary services gratis, a steady stream of gunshot victims from the low-income projects provided a reliable cash flow of drug money and ensured a tidy profit. Because of the housing projects—twenty years old and falling apart, built as they were with much-abused tax-dollars— North Jefferson Avenue was no longer a safe neighborhood, but Sal Almonde probably kept his offices there for a variety of intelligent reasons. North Jefferson was close to City Hall and police head quarters, and Almonde worked his Mafioso magic at both places. Moreover, the location provided easy access to an entrance ramp to the Interstate 95 drug corridor, and it gave Almonde a way to monitor the traffic flow between New York City and points north. Plus, being that close to the rat-infested squalor that housed so many of his best drug-addict customers probably made the guy feel like he could simply reach out to touch a throbbing vein—to take the pulse of the market so to speak.

It was more or less common knowledge that Sal was in his office from two to five every day, between his health club workout and his dinner reservation at either the Ocean Bay Grill or the Medici Lounge—the only decent eateries left downtown, unless of course, you counted the Greek diners, which were numerous and cheap enough, and served breakfast around the clock, with scrambled eggs, homefries, and a bottomless cup of coffee—all for only a couple of bucks.

Thinking hard had made me hungry again, but already I was running late, so I didn't stop to eat fried eggs. A big part of me kept hoping Sal Almonde would be gone before I got there. I was pulling into an asphalt parking lot when I finally put the obvious together. I drove around the funeral home a few times to scope out the place. There were practical reasons too, but Almonde worked above a funeral home because it gave him an edge. Even the dumbest gang banger could understand such symbolism. Mr. Almonde was in charge of death. I wondered if he had thought this out—I wouldn't put it past him. Not someone who used Lorrie for a shrink. Nevertheless, the insight might work as an ice-breaker. Something clever I could use.

Finally, I parked, and ignoring the main entrance, I went up the side steps of a fire escape, knocked on a glass-paneled French door, and was admitted into a room with ivory drapes that reached the floor and thick white carpet so spotless it made me nervous to walk on it. There were two polished mahogany desks, one on each side of the room. The door had been opened by a large, heavyset man in a dark, three-piece suit; behind him stood a smaller, wiry-looking man in a gray two-piece. Both men wore white shirts, striped ties with a lot of cranberry in them, and black leather shoes, highly shined. Their suit jackets looked a little large, and I suspected that extra cloth covered their shoulder holsters.

The hell of it was I knew both men—not well, but well enough. The big man was Geno Valenti and the little guy was Tony Bosco. I'd gone to Catholic elementary school with both of them, and Geno had been a creep—even way back then: the kind of kid that tortures frogs with sharpened sticks and crams cherry bombs into the rectums of kittens. Bosco was clearly the smarter of the two. He even looked rather clever. He moved quickly and wore steel-rimmed eyeglasses, and he still had an athletic physique. Back in elementary school he'd been a numbers runner for the Nomad Bar—I'd placed a bet or two with him myself. It was also rumored he'd hot-wired a substitute teacher's car that had disappeared into the East Side chop shops. After eighth grade graduation we'd lost touch although I'd seen him around town once in the early 1990s. He'd been riding a huge Japanese motorcycle and wearing a black Darth Vader helmet with a kind of casual flair that let you know it was nothing but costume. Now, he was wearing custom-tailored Italian suits and working for Sal Almonde, and I had the funny feeling I was meeting a long lost goomba.

I gave Geno a nod. He seemed unhappy to see me and too dumb to conceal it.

"Here to see the boss," I said to Bosco.

"So maybe that's me," he said.

Geno looked at him, slack-jawed.

"Sal Almonde," I said softly.

"He ain't here," Geno said. He was dumb enough to lie to people who knew better. I glared at him, but he didn't blink. He was well over six feet tall, overweight, and balding far worse than I was, but he had a pockmarked chin and pimples on his nose like a teenager.

"Who wants to see him?" he said finally.

"Smart," I said to Bosco, and tapped my head.

"What?" said a voice. It boomed over an intercom to a speaker on one of the desks. There was a door to an inner office, and, unlike the outside door, this one was thick and windowless and made of plated steel. It had been painted a pale beige, probably to soften the vault-like effect.

Bosco pressed a button. "Guy wants to see you, Mr. Almonde."

The heavy door opened slightly to reveal a man in a blue wool fisherman's sweater and faded but well-pressed jeans. Except for his wrinkled face, he seemed to be in excellent shape. There was a bounce to his walk and his handshake was warm and firm. His hair was thick and gray and so curly he might even have had it permed. Even in casual attire Almonde looked successful—like old, well-invested country-club money— although I knew better. He looked me over. He didn't seem surprised.

"You wanted to see me?"

"I'm Pete Lombardo," I said. "But I guess you knew that. Is there someplace we can talk in private?"

He gestured with his arm. "These are my trusted associates," he said.

I looked to Bosco and Geno, but they didn't react. "Yeah," I said.

"Gentlemen," Almonde said. I raised my arms. Geno came closer and frisked me.

"Cheap thrills," I said to Bosco.

"Clean," Geno said.

"You'll have to excuse our little rituals," Almonde said. "Safety first." He turned and I followed him into his office. The steel door closed behind us with a thud. It was like entering a meatlocker. The designer furniture was overpadded but modern. Above the walnut wainscoting were hanging bookshelves made of plate glass. Almonde took a seat behind a gleaming gold-colored desk. A tiny clean-air machine hummed away as it caught microscopic particles of dust.

"You wanted privacy," he said.

"You already knew who I was."

He shrugged, but I took that as affirmation.

"I got holes in my Escort," I said.

Almonde smiled. "So you got shit for transportation. Maybe it's all that de-icer the city throws on the road."

"Sal," I said. "It was specialty ammo. Five or six bucks a load. Not something your average gang member would spray."

"Mr. Almonde to you," he said, but he continued to smile. His teeth were so white and regular I knew they'd all been capped.

"Hey, Mr. Almonde, did you ever consider the symbolism of working above a funeral parlor?" I asked him. It got to be a better and better question the more I thought about it.

Almonde have me a long look, then smiled again to let me know he had. "You got something more to offer?" he asked.

"I think you ordered me hit."

"Everybody's got problems."

"Expensive ammo works wonders, Sal," I said. "You've probably outlived yours."

He smiled and showed me both sides of his manicured hands. His fingernails were certainly clean.

"So why'd you order me hit?"

He swiveled briefly so that he stared at his bookshelves and not at me, and when he turned back his face was a mask with a smile so serene it could have been sewn on a corpse. "So who got hit," he said. "If I ordered you hit, don't you think you'd be hit— hypothetically speaking?"

I considered this. His command of the subjunctive wasn't nearly as well developed as Mrs. McLean's, but it worked just as well. And it *was* possible I'd been shot at simply to scare me. If so, it had worked. High velocity shells maintained a wonderfully straight trajectory, but it would take utter nonchalance and telescopic sights to miss a moving target by inches, and I wasn't sure I wouldn't rather take my chances with somebody far less accurate. Or maybe I already had.

"Maybe somebody missed," I said.

Almonde seemed to lose patience. "Believe what you want."

"I'd like to believe nobody would shoot at me—not ever—for reason."

He smiled his death mask smile again. "So you know your business?" he said.

"Yeah," I said. "What little there is of it."

"Then mind your business."

"Look, Sal," I said. "I've got no beef with your organization. I'd just prefer to know there's a problem before somebody tries to solve it—permanently."

"You don't unbury the dead," Almonde said. He hesitated as if he were seeking exactly the right words. "It's disrespectful."

This hesitation was the first opening I'd seen. "Hey, man, I hear you wept over *The Godfather*."

His face registered shock, but only briefly, a twitch that let me know I'd stung him, but it passed and he was smiling again so that a part of me wondered if I'd imagined it. "She tell you that?"

"Only that," I said." But you'd better find yourself another shrink."

"You threatening me?"

"Could I?"

"What's she to you?"

"Lorrie's my girlfriend," I said.

Almonde smiled, then seemed to relax again, and I knew I'd blundered somehow.

"Like a daughter to me," he said, and grinned.

"I don't want her knowing you. You might tell her things that could get her dead."

Almonde seemed offended. "Nobody touches Lorrie," he said. "She's under my protection."

"Better not tell her that," I said. "She thinks she's a feminist."

"Why? Aren't you supposed to be honest with your therapist?"

"Never mind that shit," I said. "Better find yourself a priest if you feel a yearning to confess."

"I'm not an especially religious man," he said softly. Then he turned away from me again and drew a book from his shelves and opened it to a bookmarked page and began to read aloud. "This is your eternal life," he said. He closed the book on his finger. "Capeesh?"

"Nietzsche," I said.

"Well, that's exactly right," he said. He looked surprised.

"I'm not rich, but I'm not stupid."

"So you've read Nietzsche?" he asked me.

"Better stick to armored ammo if you want to impress me."

"So lay off the McLean stuff," he said. "Or I'll show you fear and loathing."

"Trembling," I said. "Kierkegarrd. Trembling not loathing. You must not have read him yet."

Almonde seemed genuinely amused. "You got big cojones, pal."

"Some people think so."

"You're also the little dickhead who made that porno movie."

"Jesus, I was nineteen years old," I said. "That was a long, long time ago. Besides, I only directed it. I didn't star in it."

"Yeah," Almonde said. "Big cajones, small rod. You got the brains to know better, yet you persist in thinking about me as some kind of crime boss."

"Walks like a duck."

Almonde laughed so hard he had to hold his abdomen, but he suddenly seemed to lose all patience with me. He stood up and walked toward the metal door as if to tell me our little interview was over.

"So, keep your nose clean," he said. "I might make a place for you. I employ a lot of people."

"A lot of people are after me to switch professions. Lorrie thinks I could be a shrink. My old man thinks I should get a job with the Federal government. You want to turn me into a career criminal."

Almonde roared. "A career criminal, he says!" He laughed until tears welled in his eyes. He opened the door.

"So you're warning me off?" I said. I said it loud enough to let Geno and Bosco hear.

"Quick," he said. "Hold that thought." He checked his watch as if to suggest he'd already spent too much time with me. "If I were you I'd be taking me a little vacation by tomorrow. Florida's nice this time of year."

"In-season rates," I said. "I work for a living."

Almonde hesitated. His eyes were almost colorless. "So how much would it cost you to take a short vacation?"

"That's what credit cards are for," I said. I gave Geno a thumbs-up to confuse him as I went out.

CHAPTER *15*

I'd done some of my most grueling detective work in Bridgewater's laundromats—I'd deduced the entire sad lives of other patrons from the evidence in one coin-operated washload. Of course, I'd heard it said that all-night laundromats were a great place to meet willing women, and knew from experience that was true if your tastes ran to neglected young mothers with cracked plastic laundry baskets full of blue-jeans and t-shirts and kid's shit-stained BVDs. But I'd been avoiding such places lately. Imagining the lives they led wasn't especially difficult, but it made my stomach churn. Before I'd started seeing Lorrie regularly and was consequently more desperate, there'd been times I was so hung up, or horny, or simply lonely that I'd willingly slap bellies with almost anybody. Many a time I'd shown up at the Suds-n-Duds with my box of Tide to play dumb and ask their advice about hot water or how tight to pack it in.

Most of the women had seemed frightened by me, or else flattered but noncommittal. They'd exchange knowing glances; I'd want to run away and hide; I'd swear to myself that this was absolutely the last time, that I'd buy myself a used washer and dryer or simply haul my laundry to my father's place and do it there. I had all but convinced myself that the great laundromat lay was nothing but the stuff of urban folklore, but then I'd gotten lucky— if you could call it that.

One rainy night last summer, on a starless evening when the sky was nothing but moving banks of darkness without a moon, I'd chanced into a quickie in the back seat of my Escort with a perfume-counter salesgirl from a Caldor's Discount Store. She had bad breath that smelled of cigarettes and a crotch like the throwaway peppermints that come with the check in a cheap Mexican restaurant. We picked a dark corner of the nearly deserted parking lot, the windows fogged, and the inside of the car felt like a hothouse for orchids. Neither of us undressed. I unzipped. She hiked up her denim mini-skirt and pulled her white nylon panties to one side. She was a tiny woman—ninety pounds and not quite five feet tall. For a second or so I could barely find an opening, but with one wiggle and then another, and a little spittle for lubrication, I got in. For me, it was like sex with a plastic blow-up doll, but she had already folded her own wash and urged me to finish fast because her husband was home watching the kids. I complied, and afterwards, before I'd even zipped myself up again, she'd jumped out of the car and disappeared into darkness.

Later, when I returned to the Suds-n-Duds to pop a few more quarters into a dryer, I'd sniffed my fingers and wondered if I'd imagined the whole thing. I couldn't for the life of me figure her out. Halitosis notwithstanding, she'd been young and not especially bad-looking—a pixie, a nymph from a treeless urban forest. Whatever gratification she'd sought from that flabby-bellied stranger, who just so happened to be me, had little or nothing to do with physical pleasure. Over the next couple of months, I'd twice had myself tested for a variety of communicable diseases. Everything was negative. Yet my normally rock-solid sense of reality had been undermined, and ever since I'd had the strangest thoughts in washeterias. I'd pondered the metaphysical essence of laundry—tossed and wet, real and unreal. I'd asked myself haunting questions about the fabric of space-time. Was human existence nothing more than an undarned tubesock in the dirty laundry hamper of a bachelor god?

After my chat with Almonde and company I'd driven home to warm some microwave fish sticks and canned ravioli. One of the reasons I ate so much fast food was that I'd never learned to cook.

I found my little yellow tiled kitchen depressing: the old kitchen counter had so much brown crud between the grouting that it seemed grossly unsanitary. Avocado colored kitchen appliances had come with the attic apartment, and neither my ancient one-door refrigerator nor my three-burner gas stove had ever been properly cleaned—I certainly hadn't bothered. The aluminum racks inside the little fridge were pitted and oxidized, my stove burners were splattered, and the oven so encrusted with burned-on grease that it looked like a museum piece nobody would want to own. Consequently, most of my meal preparation involved heating things in the microwave, which had a loose door and was probably leaking radiation.

As I heated my fish sticks on a paper plate I thought about the final scene in that old movie about Madame Curie, the climax where she finally isolates radium, a green glow in the darkness. Sometimes Lorrie Moore reminded me of Madame Curie—that same fearlessness and determination, not to mention a great body and the kind of independence and poise that results when they ship you off early to good boarding schools and then on to Bennington. Meeting Lorrie had been the best thing that had ever happened to me. Not only had I managed to become a bit more sexually selective, but I even got to eat a good meal once in a while. Lorrie was a gourmet cook, albeit a vegetarian, and although there was some times a little too much tofu and brown rice and organic broccoli in her pantry to suit me, it was pretty healthy stuff. Lorrie wasn't the soul food type, but her counters were always spotless. Her faucet handles gleamed; there wasn't a crumb in her toaster oven. There were certainly no splatters on her stove or kitchen walls. She'd make somebody a good wife if she ever got past the notion that most men were emotional cripples seeking to repress her. Not that she was altogether wrong about that.

Anyway, I'd gagged down my ravioli and fish sticks and put together a big wash. If I was going on vacation tomorrow, I wanted a suitcase of freshly laundered clothes. Most of what I owned in the way of clothing was churned like a compost pile and in various states of decomposition. My wardrobe wasn't extensive to begin with— which drove Lorrie crazy. She said there was no need for me to look like a bum, that my refusal to dress like an adult had something to do with my expectations of failure and negative self-image. Not that I especially cared. Usually, I only met with my clients once or twice, because if I didn't produce immediate results I didn't keep that client long. That would probably be the outcome with the McLean case. I wasn't about to get myself shot for some dead politician's widow. If that made me an unscrupulous coward, so be it.

Tonight the laundromat was nearly empty, and I didn't especially want to think about death or about sex—although of course I thought about both. A ruddy-faced young woman with streaks of gray in her spiked hair and lots of sunburned flab hanging from her upper arms was busy folding cloth diapers on an aqua-colored plastic table. She was wearing a tight sleeveless T-shirt to show off her tattoos and nipple rings, and she kept muttering to herself. The only other customer was a middle-aged Greek priest in a black wool overcoat. He was using all eight working dryers, air-fluffing what on first glance had seemed to me to be funeral shrouds but on closer examination proved to be dozens of white heavy-duty moving quilts.

I decided I could risk leaving my wet laundry in the washer with those two solid citizens while I dashed down the block to buy a bottle of Canadian whiskey. My imagination was overly active, and my stomach needed settling. I would have preferred to stay home and watch TV and maybe smoke some mild grass, but didn't have any left and didn't want to have to drive around town trying to score on some street corner.

In a package store a few doors down, an old man with liver-spotted hands sold me the whiskey. His name was Al—or anyway I'd once heard another customer call him that. I watched Al shuffle slowly around the counter to fetch my purchase. On his feet he wore fleece-lined bedroom slippers that he'd slit with a razor blade to relieve pressure on his bunions. He had a time-ravaged face, a bulbous red nose, and snow-white hair reduced to wisps. When he made change his hands seemed to shake with a kind of palsy. Al reminded me of Robert Frost, long dead, but who I'd seen once on TV. He had that kind of self-possession. Dignity in old age, or what passed for dignity in Bridgewater. For all I knew, Al might even possess some wisdom, if only "the wisdom to know the difference" as in the Alcoholics Anonymous creed. Actually, I didn't really know the guy, given that all our transactions had been commercial ones.

"How you doing, Al? Cold night out there."

He shook his head. "I got me a .357 Magnum behind this counter and the next son of a bitch tries to rip me off, I'm going to fuck him up."

"Happy trails," I told him. I grabbed my brown paper bag and left.

CHAPTER *16*

The next day I was up early. As was usual in the morning I was optimistic for reasons I didn't understand and didn't immediately care to consider. So I took myself out to breakfast. Feed a cold, starve a depression, indulge a manic high. I had a cheap whiskey hangover, a death threat from the mob, damp laundry to fold, and those holes in my Escort to deal with—but I also had Mrs. McLean's retainer, which meant I could live the examined life—if and when I decided to.

There were a lot of things wrong with Bridgewater, none of which I could do anything about. But there was also a preponderance of decent places to eat breakfast, most of them conveniently close. I picked Leon's diner on Yale Avenue where for $2.95 I clogged my arteries with soft scrambled eggs, buttered toast, homefries, a large sausage patty with too much pepper in it, and about nine cups of coffee lightened with ultra-pasteurized half-and-half. At the register, I left the waitress a wrinkled dollar that some would-be illustrator had inked over so as to turn George Washington's face into a woman's crotch. It didn't even produce a thank-you.

Yesterday already seemed like the crusty residue of a wet dream, and, upcoming vacation or not, I had chores to do today. Five faxes from various Bridgewater realtors had come in on my office machine overnight, and I had five houses to photograph for the county MLS so they could appear online and in the weekly real-estate supplement. Mrs. McLean's check was a very nice thing to have, but it seemed destined to be a one-time thing. Those MLS photos were my bread and butter, worth thirty-five bucks apiece.

I also intended to stop by the Auto Palace and buy myself a tub of Bondo to patch the bullet holes in my Escort. Fortunately, it hadn't rained last night and today was brisk—bitter cold but dry. Most of the dead leaves seemed to have blown off the trees, and even the usual smog seemed to have cleared a bit. I wondered if Mrs. Mclean would balk if I put the Bondo on my expense account.

The guy behind the parts counter in the Auto Palace was a droopy-eyed Italian named Mickey, a nervous little man in neatly pressed corduroys. I'd gotten to know him a little over the years. When you drive an old American-made car in Bridgewater, you get on pretty familiar terms with the staff in such places. Over the last three months I'd bought a starter, a rebuilt water pump, an alternator, a distributor cap, ignition wires, lug nuts, a washer-pump, a key-locking gas cap to replace one somebody had stolen, and a new heater core. I'd been in and out of the Auto Palace so often that Mickey had started giving me the twenty-percent mechanic's discount. I'd always done most of my own work on my cars, not only because I sort of instinctively knew how to, but also because although I'd lived in Bridgewater all my life, I had yet to find an honest garage.

"Doing a little body work on the side?" Mickey asked as I carried the jumbo-sized can to the metal counter. He gave me a leer.

"No, man, I spread it on whole wheat toast."

"Funny," Mickey said, awkward, as he rang it up.

I sighed. "You know anything about body putty, Mickey?"

"What's to know?"

"Can I use this stuff to patch a bullet hole?"

He was completely nonplussed, a Bridgewater native. "How big a bullet hole?"

"I got a selection. Say a couple of exit holes as big as my fist."

He shook his head. "Not when it's this cold. You need to find yourself a piece of screen and built it up in layers. A little at a time or else it shrivels and shrinks and falls out or else it bubbles up and looks like shit."

"Doesn't matter. My car already looks like shit."

"So when you gonna buy yourself a new ride?"

I rubbed my fingers together. To get the mechanic's discount I was willing to play along. One of the boys, a working stiff.

Mickey shook his head again. "And you call yourself a private investigator right?"

"That's me."

"So how come you don't investigate how all these moulinyams buy Escalades?"

I hesitated. I'd been a lot of different nasty things over the years with a lot of different nasty people, but I wasn't about to encourage Mickey—twenty-percent discount or no twenty-percent discount.

"Most people buy cars on time."

"Time shit," Mickey said. "I'm on my feet here fifty hours a week, and my wife goes play bingo every goddamn night. I get home from work. She wants me to watch the kids while she goes play bingo or runs off to the laundroamat."

I had a sudden strange sinking feeling that the salesgirl from the Suds-n-Duds might have been Mickey's wife, but that kind of coincidence wasn't possible—or was it?

"She ever win at bingo?" I asked him, simply to keep things going.

Mickey scoffed." She plays too many cards. You play too many cards you can't keep track. Besides, they got that shit fixed. You play too many cards how you gonna come out ahead?"

I worked to straight-face it. "Somebody must win sometime, I suppose."

"If she wins she don't tell me about it," Mickey said. "So far as I heard she don't ever win. I don't even know nobody that wins."

"If it bothers you that much, maybe you ought to ask her to stop," I said, still hoping we weren't having the conversation I feared we were having.

He looked exasperated. "I can't tell her nothing!"

"I guess some people don't really listen," I said.

"So you want to make a few bucks off this or what?"

I shrugged, confused. I certainly hadn't been expecting a business proposition. "I'm listening."

Mickey drew a deep breath. "Say somebody was to snatch her purse at the bingo place. Scare her bad. Make her piss her big pink bloomers. Maybe then she won't gamble so much."

I smiled and shook my head. I wasn't sure what I felt but it wasn't good.

"In the parking lot," Mickey said. "She wears those shoulderbags— you know, with the long leather straps."

"I don't know if I'm up to purse snatching, Mickey."

"So what's to be up to? You get caught, give me a call. I'll tell the cops I know you."

I hesitated. Part of me was actually considering it. The problem with life at the bottom margins was that there was always something a little lower, a little worse.

"Come on," Mickey said. "I'll pay you a hundred bucks. And you need a buddy in the parts business if you're gonna drive beaters."

I experienced a kind of momentary rage and felt myself grit my teeth, but it passed like a fog and I wasn't sure why I'd felt it. For a second or so I hated myself, I hated Mickey, and I hated life in general. So much for the lingering effects of a decent breakfast.

"How would I even know her?"

"You see her once you'd never forget her," Mickey said and pulled out his wallet to show me. "She weighs nearly three hundred pounds."

It wasn't quite relief that I experienced. I had a strange visionary moment where I saw myself once again with the tiny woman in the car and then a new imagined scene where I was swinging a three-hundred-pound lady around and around by the straps of a shoulderbag she refused to relinquish, around and around until she was almost weightless, circling faster and faster in the Knights of Columbus parking lot, the circles getting larger and wider and the woman floating higher and higher until she was straining like a helium-filled blimp against a thin restraining line.

"Let it go," I said aloud.

"What?"

"Sorry, Mickey." I picked up my can of Bondo and left abruptly. I saw he was disappointed, and he had every right to be.

Inadvertently, I'd led him on. Shit on that. Sooner or later he'd recruit somebody to snatch her purse. Half the unemployed teenagers in Bridgewater would jump at the chance, but for a while anyway I could afford to refuse some jobs. I might be only one rung up from the bottom, but it was an important rung. I had houses to photograph.

CHAPTER *17*

The first two houses were easy shoots, vacant Cape Cods on side streets off Peak Avenue, just north of the Dollar-Value Theater, which, many long years and once-upon-a-time ago had occasionally screened independent and foreign and sometimes classic films, and had been the closest thing Bridgewater had ever had to an art house, and which, for purely sentimental and idiosyncratic reasons, always reminded me of my father's all-time favorite movie, *Dr. Zhivago*, which, he reminded me every time we drove by, he'd seen there once, as a new release, and which I, as a kid, whenever it was playing on late night TV, he'd always allow me to stay up to watch along with him—even if the movie started at midnight and ended at three a.m. and I had to miss school the next day. My mother had never approved, but it had become a kind of masculine bonding ritual, something we had between us, engendering a kind of closeness we didn't ordinarily share, and as a kid I'd thought those corny shots of the ice-shrouded winter palace were the loveliest things I'd ever seen.

For an Army brat from inner-city Bridgewater all that frozen Siberian countryside had seemed the finer stuff of other people's dreams. All was white and gossamer and lace. There wasn't a greasy dumpster, nor a car-exhaust-blackened snowbank, nor a cancer-eaten stop sign anywhere. Even the soldiers on horseback had seemed romantic, breathing warm steam clouds that hung in that frigid air. Red army, white army—I didn't give a crap. Either army seemed a lot more appealing than my father's olive-drab army—or the corrugated metal flight hangar in South Bridgewater where he had his green steel desk.

Now that hangar was a place that got cold in the winter. It was impossible to heat an un-insulated metal building—especially one large enough to shelter the huge attack helicopters that passed for contemporary cavalry. They'd ship the choppers in by freighter, forwarded from the Persian Gulf, damaged military aircraft beat to shit by the desert sands. After hours of brutal flight time, my father would be there to make sure the indifferent civil-service mechanics tore down those helicopter rotorheads completely and checked the tolerances of every single precision part before they slapped a sticker on the fuselage and shipped things back to the Middle East.

All winter long, repair crews would huddle around roaring salamanders to warm their hands over flames fed by waste-oil and worn transmission and hydraulic fluids. Work went slowly in the cold. And my father was often appalled that some of the civilians who worked on the choppers were less than enthusiastic about repairing gunships. A few even went so far as to flash peace signs at one another as they torqued down the engine bolts. "I don't give a damn if you think we should be over there or not," he would say. "Those are red-blooded American lives!"

The Cape Cods were vacant now, as were so many lower-middle-class homes in Bridgewater these days. Taxes were high and property values had plummeted. Many marginally employed families had mailed their house keys to the banks that held their mortgages and walked away. My job was to take the pictures quickly before local kids tossed loose bricks through the windows or tore out the copper pipe or BX cable to sell for scrap. Today neither of the two houses was in especially bad condition yet, but I doubted either would find a buyer. Both were asbestos-sided and needed paint, and there was no way to rent them for enough to cover taxes and interest payments. The entire neighborhood was going downhill fast. Many of the houses had un-mowed yards and untrimmed shrubbery where creeps could hide, and I'd seen tiny plastic bags in the gutters along those streets.

I backed up to get a good clear shot. Five rooms, one bath, and a basement with a six-foot ceiling. Levittown-sized houses but built of cheaper materials and without the common-sense design that allowed room for future expansion. Every time I took pictures of small vacant homes, it made me sadder than a frozen slush pile in December. Bridgewater certainly had its share of homeless folk and winter was coming fast. I thought about that homeless family that had fried in the train station fire. A long run of bad luck and it could happen to anybody. Even me.

Suddenly I felt ice cold. I got back into my Escort and cranked the heater up to high as I drove away. The next house on my list was out on Midland Beach, not quite in Bridgewater proper but close in enough for the listing to be somewhat desirable—not only because it was right on the water but because the taxes were lower. "Charming oceanfront bungalow," the description read. And I was probably expected to photograph it so that it looked like one. "Tenant occupied." Which likely meant it was a shack. Nine or ten gay fraternity boys from Yale had probably sublet it as a winter retreat. They could watch fist-fucking films and listen to the sea's slow melancholy roar at night. The tides would rise and ebb as they slept beneath fishnets and mummified glitter-glued starfish, three or four to a moldy bed.

I could make myself sadder than shit, I realized, anytime I wanted to. Bridgewater certainly provided the raw material for an extended depression if I wanted to wallow. Staying clear of such moods was harder to do, but I was determined to try. The sea at least looked clean—but the white-capped waves rolled in to meet an oil-slicked shoreline, a tideline marked with broken shells and scraps of pressure-treated lumber, medicine bottle caps, and plastic six-pack rings—the kind that strangle seagulls.

I got out of the car and snapped the picture, keeping my focus shallow to turn the background into a romantic blur. It was a small house but neatly kept; it had a small picket-fenced yard, and a front porch weathered to the color of silver. White sheets and pillowcases billowed on a clothesline. A charming one-bedroom oceanfront bungalow. Whoever was renting it probably weren't fraternity boys after all. Things were never as bad as I imagined. I stood in the sand-blown street and snapped another shot from a different angle. All considered, it was a quaint, homey kind of place—fit for a neurotic hermit should I ever become one. Quaint, rustic, and on the ocean, and priced to sell for four-hundred-sixty-nine thousand dollars.

I climbed back into my Escort and took off. The next house on my list was out by Saugamore Reservoir, twenty minutes on the Merritt Parkway but light years from Bridgewater in almost every other way. Saugamore, Connecticut, was the New England of postcards and calendars, the Connecticut of covered bridges that I sometimes forgot existed. Saugamore had Christmas tree farms and fresh air and white birches and even an overgrown apple orchard or two. The only problem was it cost a two-hundred thousand per undeveloped acre and nothing was sold in less than three-acre lots. And that for worn-out farmland without even a tumbledown barn to hide your spare yacht in.

By these standards, the place on my list seemed like a real bargain. Three point four acres with a tiny A-framed chalet for nine-hundred-seventy thousand. Not bad, but then again, real estate sales were always slower around the holidays. I slammed my car door and stood by a mailbox atop a stone wall and tried shooting the chalet. The real problem was light. Huge pines lined both sides of the narrow road. Also, I wanted that stone wall in the foreground. I might not be the best detective in the world, but I wasn't a bad photographer—even with only a digital camera to work with. There was no telling what I might have become if I hadn't made that porno-flick—not that I regretted it. Hell, I had nothing against giving a customer honest value, strange as that notion might seem to most citizens of Bridgewater.

I continued to play with the optical zoom adjustment on my camera, trying for something utterly lovely I knew I could never capture. I took four or five quick shots, but the wind was icy and I was getting ready to give up and get back in my Escort when the front door of the chalet opened and a young, dark-haired woman came down the soggy path. There were round concrete stepping stones that led towards the mailbox. I stood there and watched her come, jumping from stone to stone as if she were crossing an icy stream. She was a very pretty girl, somewhere in her early twenties. Her windblown hair was long and her eyes very heavy-looking, outlined with black mascara, but otherwise her features were soft. She was wearing a short gray Bolivian sweater of raw clumpy wool over black stretch tights and ankle-high snap boots with pointed toes. It wasn't enough clothing for this kind of cold, and she had pulled her arms up inside the sleeves of the bulky sweater, folding her arms to hug herself like a woman in a straightjacket.

"Can I help you?" she asked as she got closer.

"Taking photos of the house for the MLS."

"Oh," she said softly, and she sounded disappointed, "I thought you might be an interested buyer."

I shrugged. "When did you list it?"

"Yesterday."

"A little early," I said, and smiled. "It hasn't even made the hot-sheets yet."

"Did you get a good picture? Be sure to get a good picture."

"Not quite enough light," I confessed.

"Did you try it by the back door?" she asked. "It's nicer out that way."

I hesitated. "Better show me."

She turned and I followed and studied her as she moved. I was certainly getting shown. The stretch tights below her sweater's hem left nothing to my imagination.

We had just turned the corner into the chalet's backyard when a dog began to bark, an Irish setter or maybe a setter mix. As I came into view, the dog went wild. It was chained to a pine tree, and the chain had wrapped around the trunk and worn the bark away, ringing the tree completely—it would be dead by spring. There was an oversized doghouse with a cedar-shake roof like the one on the chalet's, but the dog didn't use it for shelter because there was a dirt hole under the doghouse floor that it clearly preferred instead. Piles of mushy turds surrounded the tree, and a stainless steel dog bowl lay upside down on a patch of soggy bare earth.

"Oh," she said. "I forgot about the dog. I never go near him."

"Does he bite?"

"He's my boyfriend's dog," she said as if this were some kind of answer.

I shook my head.

"Is the light better here?" she asked.

It was better, I supposed; there was even a little seasonal stream that would photograph quite well if you could ignore the dog. The problem was I couldn't ignore the dog. It continued to strain against the chain. The barking seemed more like a whine now.

"Maybe the dog's thirsty," I said.

"It's my boyfriend's dog," she repeated and dropped her eyes. "Actually, we're separating as soon as we sell the house."

"So where's he at?"

"Out of town," she said. "On business."

I moved a little closer to the doghouse and reached gingerly for the metal bowl, drawing it from the mud, half afraid the dog would snap. It cowered in a way that let me know it expected to be beaten. I carried the bowl to the tiny stream and rinsed it and dipped it full and carried it back and set it down. The dog lapped up the water greedily, so when it was empty, I got it another.

The young woman stood there and hugged herself and watched me. The dog came closer and I rubbed its ears and walked it around the tree until I had untangled most of its chain. The wind was colder than ever.

"Tell your boyfriend to water his dog," I said.

"So aren't you going to take another photo? I think you should take another photo?"

"Up your ass," I said, and watched until her face registered shock. Then I turned, and kept on going.

I had one more house to photograph, but first I wanted some lunch. It was early to eat—only eleven o'clock or so—but I took the Main Street exit off the Parkway and drifted down to the McDonald's and ordered a quarter-pounder without the cheese and a large coffee with one cream. All that cold air had given me an appetite, but I was still trying to cut back on the extra fat. Dead meat. There was a playground inside the McDonald's with a bunch of little kids bobbing around on grotesque plastic animals mounted on heavy-duty coil springs. I watched them for a while and sipped my coffee, savoring it, giving it full attention like a student of Zen trying to stay focused. All morning long I'd been running from myself. Saint Peter of Lombardo, the patron saint of dogs. All morning long I'd been avoiding some hard questions. Was I going to let Sal Almonde scare me off the McLean investigation? What assurance did I have that he wouldn't try killing me again anyway? These were damn hard questions. Also, in good conscience, could I take Mrs. McLean's money for doing nothing? But I didn't necessarily need to be operating in good conscience—or did I?

I wasn't sure other private investigators faced these moral dilemmas. Nobody I knew did. No wonder Lorrie had tried to talk me into going back to college. She seemed to think I'd make a good psychotherapist, but she was wrong about that. I didn't have the patience for it. I couldn't imagine listening to other people's craziness all day long. I could barely stand to listen to my own.

I stood up and dumped my tray's worth of plastic trash. It would either be incinerated and poison the air or else endure in some clay-capped landfill for the next ten thousand years. I went out to my Escort. The day was clouding up a little, but the wind seemed to have died. My last stop was on Linden Street. I coasted down the hill to Linden, turned left again, and looked for the Realtor's sign outside a two-family three story. I found it, stopped, got out, and snapped off two quick shots. I didn't even bother turning off the engine. Making a house like that look good was an impossible task. It was an ugly green color, aluminum sided on the front with stucco on the sides and back. There were gratings on the lower-story windows and bent-out-of-shape aluminum awnings on the upper story. An utterly ugly house, but at a hundred and sixty thousand, far below tax value, it would probably be snapped up. A big old place like that could be cut into four or five small apartments and depreciated so as to generate a positive cash flow. It was the kind of investment of which my father would approve: solid, sensible, and not at all appealing to me.

CHAPTER *18*

The blue Buick behind me had crushed blue upholstery—I'd bet anything on it. There are things you know instinctively. Others you know by means of tutored intuition. And I knew with a perverse certainty that the upholstery in that Buick was blue. What I didn't know for certain was who was behind the wheel, or why I was being followed.

So far as I could tell by sneaking glances in the rear view mirror, there were two men in business suits—Geno and Bosco probably—but their windshield was dark tinted, and I couldn't see their faces. They stayed a dozen or so car lengths back, but most of the time there wasn't even another car between us, so I began to suspect I was meant to know about the tail. If my Escort had really been shot full of holes simply to show how easy it would be to kill me, perhaps I was being followed to determine if I'd learned my lesson.

I decided to find out and mashed down the accelerator. Immediately, I could sense confusion behind me. I took a hard left turn, squealing my recapped tires across two lanes of traffic, then I circled the block and slowed down so they could catch me, then hit the gas and roared up Main street. When I coasted to a stop at the red light at the intersection by Pathmark, the Buick pulled up beside me on the left, and I gave Geno and Bosco a smile and a friendly wave.

If they had any sense at all, they would have blasted me right there, but like everybody else these days, Sal Almonde's organization was likely worried about its public image. Confronting him head-on had been a smart thing to do. I'd made him worry about what I knew and who I might have told. Consequently, I'd made him reticent about reordering a hit. That kind of hesitancy gave me an edge—which was something to use so long as I didn't push my luck. If Geno and Bosco had simply been told to watch me, I could make their lives miserable with a certain impunity.

I left the Escort running, but slid the transmission into park and got out and slammed the door and walked over to the Buick idling beside me. I rapped on the passenger window and Geno hit the automatic opener. He was in the shotgun seat and had his forearm over his eyes.

"I knew it was blue velour," I said.

"How's that?" said Bosco, who was driving.

"Never mind," I said. "How you boys doing?"

"Can't complain," Bosco said. "Another day, another Euro."

"We should carpool," I said, "since we're going the same places."

"Frankly I prefer my own vehicle," Bosco said, and for the first time I noticed he was going gray at the temples.

I shrugged. "Free country," I said. "I guess I'll be rolling along."

"So where you headed?" Geno asked.

"Home to pack a suitcase. Then back to my office to check for messages. Then to my bank to cash a check. Then to Bridgewater Airport to catch the very next flight to Florida."

"Smart move," Bosco said.

"I've been feeling disproportionately stressed," I said. "You boys zipping down to Miami to party with me?"

"Afraid not," Bosco said. "Some people got to work for a living."

I let that slide. The light had changed to green as we spoke and traffic behind the Buick had backed up. A few horns began to sound. Geno got out of the car, slowly drew a long-barreled pistol from his shoulder holster, and pointed it at the sky.

The horns stopped.

"You're scaring the tourists," I said.

Geno smiled. "I got me a gun permit," he said.

Bosco shook his head and grinned. I turned and got back into my Escort and slammed the door and headed again for home—that one-bedroom illegal attic apartment in the three-family my father owned. The steep interior stairs were hell, but they kept me from being in any worse shape than I was already, and the rent was nothing—two hundred bucks a month. Another big plus was that, in winter, free heat rose up from the roach-infested apartments below so that my utility bill was almost nil—another important consideration in a climate like Bridgewater's.

I made my way up the inside stairwell to my apartment. The downstairs landing stank of insecticide and soiled Pampers, but I climbed on through and got my door unlocked. The air inside was better. I bolted the door behind me and began packing.

Undershorts, the baggy boxer kind that Lorrie loathed. A couple of all-cotton oxford-cloth dress shirts, both with slightly frayed collars. A Walmart sweatsuit, size tall-men's extra large, that could double as either streetwear or cold-weather pajamas. A faded Speedo swimsuit—because I was supposedly going to Florida. A solid red tie. A medium weight blue suit. Old Levis. A disposable plastic razor. A toothbrush and tiny tube of Tartar-Control Crest. Dental floss that my dentist insisted I use on receding gums. Dress shoes worn down at the heels and hiking boots I'd seldom wore. A medical kit: plastic pill bottles with the prescription labels removed so nobody could figure me out by examining them, antihistamines for hay fever, twenty penicillin tablets, a tube of anti-bacterial ointment, codeine for pain, amphetamines for energy, antacids for my stomach, two sterile compress bandages, and some Band-Aid adhesive strips. Also, duct tape on a roll—the old-fashioned cloth kind that was nearly as strong as rope and could be used to fix almost anything—from a radiator hose to a broken arm. I found a pocket comb and a handful of coins in my bureau drawer, and I put these in my overcoat pocket along with a selection of used wine-bottle corks that I grabbed from the junk drawer by the kitchen sink. I took out my ring of keys and unhooked my Swiss army knife. It had a can opener, a corkscrew, a tiny magnifying glass, a nail clipper, both Phillips and regular blade screwdrivers, tiny scissors I used to clip my nose hairs, and two different-sized knife blades.

Lorrie had gotten the knife for me as a birthday present, but nowadays it wouldn't pass through the metal detectors, and since 9/11 you couldn't carry it on a plane. Besides, I was intending to carry something far more lethal.

When I was done packing, I had one terribly overstuffed carry-on—the rectangular kind with wheels and retractable handle that fits neatly in the overhead rack, plus my digital camera on a strap around my neck. I also decided I'd wear my trench coat, despite the bent belt buckle, in the hope I'd look like a harried businessman. I still felt like I was forgetting something, but I always felt that way. Lorrie said it had something to do with not being able to remember my childhood.

I walked around the apartment, checking lights and stove and faucets and jiggling the toilet handle until water stopped running. Then I found the yellow legal pad I kept by my bed to remember the nightmares that Lorrie said I conveniently forgot. The pad was three years old, but still had lots of blank paper because I was usually too lazy to write anything down. I tore off a page and left a note on the kitchen table.

> To Whom It May Concern:
> Please don't ransack my apartment. All valuables and pertinent legal information are stored elsewhere. Should you need to know my exact whereabouts while I'm vacationing, I suggest you contact my attorney.
> Best,
> Pete

After I had finished writing this out, I had to copy it over because my handwriting was illegible, but leaving the note on the table gave me a good, mildly perverse feeling. I didn't have any valuables except for some decent guns, and a lot of heavy, hard-covered novels left over from my college days, and no information—or anyway, not much. I didn't really have an attorney either, except for the incompetent public defender, but somebody might waste a lot of time finding out exactly who or what I didn't know.

CHAPTER *19*

When I went down to my Escort again with my luggage, Geno and Bosco were sitting at the curb in their Buick sipping coffee from brown paper cups and reading *Sports Illustrated*. They pointed at me and laughed when I took wine corks from my pocket and examined them until I found two of the proper size to plug the bullet holes in my roof. The Bondo job would have to wait. I gave them the finger as I pulled out into traffic, and they fell into line behind me.

The next stop was the bank's drive-in window, where, to cash Mrs. McLeans's check, I had to show two forms of photo ID to a lady with crooked teeth. Although I'd had an checking account at this same bank for nearly ten years, there was always a new teller and always the same old drill. The rigmarole with the bank put me in a bad mood, but I wanted the cash. I could use cash in ugly places where the natives didn't know from American Express.

When I pulled out of the line, Geno and Bosco were still waiting. I realized they meant to follow me to the airport. I headed instead for my office cube where I checked my fax machine for new messages—there weren't any. I cranked up my computer, down loaded the photos from my digital camera into the MLS net, and unlocked my deep-drawer army-surplus file. I drank a warm can of Miller that I'd almost forgotten I'd hidden there, swapped the cash off into a billfold loaded with fake ID, and collected a sordid assortment of weapons.

The decision to carry firearms wasn't a decision I made lightly. They were vile things—guns. The bad habit of pointing them at people was like the habit of drinking—hard to stop once you started, but with Geno and Bosco hanging around, I felt like I needed protection: a double-barreled shotgun with a folding aluminum stock, both barrels filled with the soft steel buckshot that supposedly doesn't poison ducks, a old Colt .38 revolver with a custom leather grip—an absolute classic I'd bought from a defrocked priest, and a cheap, plastic-and-ceramic *Soldier of Fortune* special—a two-shot .22 pen–sized plastic handgun that snapped apart into pieces like a child's toy and could supposedly pass though an airport X-ray machine undetected so long as the components were separated and the bullets were hidden separately.

I stuck the unloaded revolver under the driver's seat and stashed some .38 ammo and a handful of extra shotgun shells in glove compartment. I dropped one piece of the tiny plastic .22 in my satchel and another in my overcoat pockets and a third into the inside pocket of my suit. I unscrewed the battery compartment of my digital camera and carefully replaced the two tiny batteries with .22 cartridges inside hollowed out A-cells. This would make for a serious federal weapons charge if I got caught by airport security, but I didn't intend to be caught.

I tucked the shotgun under my armpit and covered it with my raincoat as I carried it downstairs to my car. Bosco and Geno didn't look amused. There was no possible way I could smuggle my serious metal guns or ammo on a plane, but I could leave them in the Escort and the Escort in long-term parking—which was probably safer than leaving them locked in my apartment when people knew I was away. Meanwhile, I felt a lot better having them along for the ride.

It wasn't a long drive. A solid twenty minutes when there wasn't traffic—except there was always traffic. I coaxed the Escort up to fifty-five, where the front-end started to shake, put an old bootleg Miles Davis tape in the cassette player to work against the high-pitched sound of wind screaming up through the exit holes that

I'd covered with rubber floor mats since they were too big to plug with corks. I tried to massage tension from my neck. I wondered if Bosco and Geno would follow me all the way onto the plane. Probably not. Unless they checked their own guns, they couldn't pass through the X-ray checkpoint, and with any luck at all I could assemble and load my hijacker's special just as soon as I got away from them. That would leave me lightly armed but highly paranoid, and I could certainly live with that.

At the airport, I stashed my shotgun under a backseat blanket, parked the Escort in the long-term lot, grabbed my coat and overnight bag, locked the car, checked the locks, and started hiking for the terminal. Bosco and Geno parked a couple of rows over and followed. They stood right behind me as I waited to buy my ticket. I looked up at them and smiled, but I was nervous enough to grit my teeth. Airports were a great place to bump a guy off. Everyone rushing around like mad. If they could catch me alone, I wouldn't need to be followed to Florida because I'd no longer be going anywhere.

I might not be worth killing so far as Almonde was concerned, but Almonde was upper management, and like all good managers he probably knew enough to delegate authority. No doubt he granted Bosco and Geno opportunities to exercise a little discretion. If I turned up dead in the Bridgewater Airport, nobody but Lorrie and my father would lose sleep over it.

I began to regret giving Bosco and Geno the finger. I thought of them as punks and bullies because I'd known them in grade school, but I'd been a pornographer at nineteen and I expected people to forget that. Geno and Bosco were men now—hard, cold, brutal men, and who, after all, was I to feel contemptuous? A private detective so unsuccessful he had trouble cashing a check at his own bank? I was as bad as Sal Almonde with his existential therapy. If I were smart, why wasn't I rich? The answer to that question seemed as elusive as a koan, and the question itself had become the mantra of my generation.

At the weigh-in counter I asked a reservations girl with a short purple hairdo about the possibility of a seat on the very next flight to Florida. She was actually kind of cute.

"Orlando, Jacksonville, Ft. Lauderdale, or Miami?"

"Miami," I said, because it would certainly arouse less suspicion if I knew where I was going.

She didn't bat an eye, but behind me I could hear Geno and Bosco snicker.

Her fingers worked a keyboard. "Sorry, Sir, there's nothing direct until tonight."

"Is anything direct these days?" This to make her smile.

She frowned instead. "I have a one-hop connecting flight through Philadelphia to Ft. Lauderdale leaving in forty minutes."

"How much is the ticket?"

"Eight-eighty-eight-fifty-one—including fees and taxes."

Expense account or no expense account, I did my best not to wince. "One way?"

She nodded.

"Perfect," I said. "Put me on the aisle."

"Open seating, Sir," she said. "Last name?"

"Lombardo," I said. "Peter."

When I saw her fingers hesitate on the keypad, I pulled out my ID with a flourish, but I almost made a mistake and handed her a Vermont driver's license, one of the out-of-state photo IDs I was carrying around with various inane names and addresses on them. After my last DUI arrest, I'd wanted to avoid any further insurance increases or points against my driving record—just in case I got stopped by the cops again—so a few months back I'd purchased a half dozen bogus out-of-state licenses for $120 in cash from a hungry-for-the business young forger who catered to Bridgewater's illegal alien population. I doubted they'd stand up to serious computerized scrutiny, but at twenty bucks apiece, I'd been unable to resist the bargain.

She stapled a ticket folder without smiling. "Gate B-1, Mr. Lombardo," she said.

I nodded. "B-one. Like the vitamin for stress."

"Luggage?" Still no smile.

"A carry-on," I said.

"Has your bag been out of your possession?"

"Nope," I said, as if I'd certainly admit this if it had.

"Anything flammable, liquid, or potentially hazardous?"

"None of the above," I lied.

She gave me my expensive ticket, and I hoisted my bag as I moved toward the escalator that rose toward the boarding gates. Geno and Bosco got out of line when I did and followed as I walked swiftly toward the X-ray checkpoint which, as I'd hoped, stopped them cold. The security people made me take off my shoes, and I caught a whiff of something foul, but my all-plastic disposable gun, which I'd already transferred in pieces to my carry-on, passed through X-ray without a hitch, and I breathed a sigh of relief. Geno and Bosco were fumbling around all over themselves. They would need to find a locker fast to stow their heavy pistols—and even unarmed they might not immediately get through. Not if security got suspicious and asked to see their boarding passes.

I had a few minutes to myself now and was determined to make the best of them. The second I was through the gate I grabbed my luggage off the conveyor belt and started to walk fast. Down the corridor and around the second bend I found what I was looking for—a men's room. I entered the corner stall and hung my luggage on the door hooks and locked the door behind me. Then I got up on the seat so my legs couldn't be seen beneath the doors. It was tight and awkward, but I unzipped my overnighter and began to assemble my weapon and load it with the ammo I'd stashed inside my camera. The interlocking plastic components snapped together around a short ceramic barrel. A worthless piece of mail-order shit—it would probably warp after a round or two, but you could fire twice and kill a man if you hit him squarely in the heart or else through an eye socket so the bullets didn't bounce off the hard bones of his skull.

It took me nearly three minutes to assemble the little gun. My heart was pounding all the while, and somebody entered the men's room about two seconds before I was done. Finally, I got it loaded.

I put the gun in my pocket and got down off the throne. Then I unlocked the door and saw Geno at the sink, squeezing a zit.

"Pimple cream is easier," I said.

He smiled at me, and his smile gave me heartburn. A second or so later Bosco came in and found us.

"Found a locker to check your firearms, gentlemen?"

"Fuck you, Lombardo," Geno said, and came up with a box-cutter on a plastic handle. So much for the X-ray checkpoints of Bridgewater Municipal Airport. Everybody and his brother-in-law was thinking like a terrorist these days—even me. But if a stupid fuck like Geno could get a box-cutter through, it gave me pause to wonder if somebody had deliberately compromised airport security by bribing the luggage screeners. But who might have something to gain from the potentially horrific consequences of lax airport security? The Pinkertons? The Greyhound Bus Company? Geno's "blade" was really nothing more than a razor-sharp metal strip, but a thing like that had helped to take down the World Trade Towers and could certainly make your face such a mess that even pimple cream wouldn't help. Bosco had backed up against the entrance door so it couldn't be opened.

"Maybe I'll cut out your fucking tongue and leave you here to bleed," Geno said.

"Maybe not today," I said, and the little gun was in my hand.

Geno looked at it and grinned, but I was pointing the barrel at his pimpled nose. "That ain't much of a piece," he said.

"It's not the gun, it's the gunner," I said. I had both hands wrapped to steady things, and my finger was on the plastic trigger. The firing pin was only being held back by two rather ordinary-looking elastic bands.

"Fuck you, Lombardo," Geno said.

"I get out or somebody gets dead," I said. "And Sal Almonde isn't pleased."

"Fuck you, Lombardo," Geno said.

"You ought to consult a shrink if you got this compulsion to repeat things. Ask Almonde to recommend one."

Bosco smiled at that. "So that skinny black bitch is your girl friend?" He gestured at Geno who looked sullen but pocketed the knife.

"Okay, okay," Bosco said. "So we bury the hatchet. You got a job. We got a job. No hard feelings."

I looked at Geno.

"Ease up," Bosco said.

Geno backed away from me, and I lowered the gun a bit, but I kept my finger on the trigger.

"You go out first."

"Everybody's on edge," Bosco said. He sounded tired.

"Yeah," said Geno. "We only wanted to make sure you got off to Florida all right."

"Fine," I said. "You go first."

They went out, I followed with the tiny gun in my pocket, and we all walked to B-1 where the connecting flight to Philly was already boarding.

"Bon voyage," Bosco said.

"I'll send you an alligator postcard from Florida," I said.

"Do that," Geno said. "You do that."

I gave the steward my ticket and went up the aluminum boarding ramp and breathed a little easier, but it wasn't until the plane had taxied away from the gate and was sitting on the tarmac revving for takeoff that I realized all the business with the weapons had been unnecessary, and I could have simply stayed public and eliminated the possibility of a showdown with Bosco and Geno. Some sick part of me had wanted to confront them, and I'd manipulated the situation so it had played itself out like that. Pretty compulsive. Pretty unbalanced. The funny thing was I sort of liked myself that way.

It was a short uneventful flight with nothing but a plastic cup of diet cola and a tiny metallic-foil package of peanuts to interrupt my thinking. In the plane's tiny restroom, I'd disassembled my little gun, wiped it for prints, dropped the two tiny bullets down the chemical toilet where you'd have to strain through human shit to retrieve them, and trashed the other plastic pieces in two different trash bins. When the plane hit the long wet runway at Philadelphia, I was already unbuckling my seatbelt and getting ready to go. Of course, that did me no good. I had to wait in line with the rest of the mutton while the plane rolled to a stop and everybody unbuckled and fiddled with the overhead compartments and pulled down luggage and bumped into everybody else.

Once we were off the plane though, I raced for the nearest ticket counter, where I tried rather impulsively to trade in the unused portion of my ticket and catch the next open flight back to Bridgewater. The girl behind the counter was a red-haired clone of the purple-haired girl back home. "I'm sorry, Sir. There's nothing flying back to Bridgewater until late tomorrow morning."

"How about the New York airports?"

She punched a few buttons. "I have one first-class seat left on a continuing flight to Newark. But there's a twelve-hour wait, and it would also be very costly—nearly nine-hundred dollars."

I tried to look unhappy and managed without much difficulty.

She smiled and punched a few more buttons.

"That's all I have," she said cheerfully. She lowered her voice a bit. "Sorry."

"Okay," I said. "Sell me a nine-hundred dollar ticket to Newark for twelve hours from now."

She typed a few numbers and the computer spit out a ticket and once again I paid for it with cash. Very conspicuous these days, but also very necessary with the maxed-out credit cards I carried. It was actually rather pleasant to think of myself as the kind of person who could so casually fly first class—what with the unlimited free drinks and larger seats.

"Gate 28-C. Check in for boarding about fifty minutes before flight time."

"Nearest bar?"

She pointed up. "Full services on Concourse C. Up the corridor and continue to your right." She smiled again.

I smiled back. Then I hoisted my luggage and headed back into the real world.

Past the exit checkpoint, onto the moving sidewalk, up the escalator, and down the wide-curved corridor, and all the way I had the strangest feeling people were watching me, but I checked my fly and found it zipped and dismissed the sensation as nerves.

There were far weirder folk than me to look at: right-to-life Baptists with throwaway pamphlets, a troop of enormously over-weight Girl Scouts who kept unfolding and refolding an American flag, an entire clan of Hassidic Jews who appeared to be suffering from Tourette's syndrome, Korean evangelicals in knock-off Nikes who seemed intent on saving the travelers of Philly with pimento-loaf sandwiches and apple cider in Dixie cups, smuggled-in Chinese workers searching for the nearest sweatshop, rain-forest advocates in polyester T-shirts, die-hard Maoists making the case for nuclear fusion.... In a crowd like that, a blue-collar private detective seemed like the thing to be. "Trippers and Askers surround me," wrote Walt Whitman, and on the New Jersey Turnpike they've named a piss-stop after him.

CHAPTER *20*

Bridgewater's airport security was one thing. Philadelphia's hopefully another. I found a storage locker to stash my heavy coat and carry-on, and suddenly I felt lightheaded and unburdened. It was almost too easy. Moving through the airport crowd without a coat or luggage, it was as if I'd shed my past and any obligation to anybody. Maybe Sal Almonde was right after all—maybe I really did need a vacation. I decided I'd reconsider my decision to return to Bridgewater over a drink or two.

I found the bar and settled down on a brown leatherette stool. It was a morose, sterile place with a middle-aged barmaid and computer-regulated nozzle on the bottle and beer taps that dripped out suds in pre-measured dollops like so much expensive medicine. There was no way for the barmaid to give away anything free to a good steady customer like I could become—at least not any way I could see.

I ordered a shot of whiskey and a cold draft beer. Both came in throwaway plastic cups like the ones they used on the planes. She served me without a word. I paid with a pair of tens, got four dollars in change, and carried the cups to the end of the bar so as not to have to listen to the country music awards show on the big screen TV.T here weren't any other customers—quite understandable since six ounces of draft beer and a splash of generic whiskey had just cost me sixteen dollars.

I tossed down the whiskey and chewed the lip of the plastic beer cup and studied the barmaid and finally remembered to ask for a receipt. She was quick and agile and efficient and married—or any way she was wearing a simple gold band. She seemed neither happy nor unhappy. Her voice betrayed no accent that could give me a clue to her ethnic or regional origin. She wore black knit slacks, a short-sleeved nylon blouse, and, except for the ring, no jewelry of any kind. Her hair was a medium brown color, and it was cut at a medium length. Her skin was pale. Her makeup was not excessive. She didn't even wear a nametag. I tried to think how I'd describe her to someone I didn't know and found that I couldn't do it. I could close my eyes and immediately forget what she looked like. She seemed nearly as impersonal as the computer regulated tap.

Sherlock Holmes himself couldn't have figured her out, but old Sherlock probably wouldn't indulge sick fantasies of smashing her bleached white teeth with the heavy bar-top ashtray and trashing her stupid professional composure. Sherlock probably wouldn't have such thoughts, much less suffer remorse for thinking them, but then the Victorians were pretty repressed. It was a good thing, I supposed, that ostensibly normal human beings couldn't read each others' minds, but I wondered if I were sending out any kind of violent vibes. I even considered telling her what I was thinking about—just to see how she'd react, but thought better of it. If I were really going back to Bridgewater I had drinking time to kill and really didn't want to need to find myself another bar.

Then I found myself thinking about Lorrie, wondering what she would make of my ugly little fantasy—probably that I either wanted to injure her—or else some anonymous female part of myself—not that I'd ever tell her about any of this. There are certain psychotic ideas that it was best to keep hidden from lovers and psycho-analysts—perhaps especially from lovers and psychoanalysts.

I was thinking so hard about all this stuff that I inadvertently drained my tiny beer and the barmaid came over and asked if I wanted another round. I stared at her blankly for a moment, then nodded and reached deep into my pocket for a quarter. "Double or nothing?"

"Sir?"

I flipped the coin in the air, caught it, slapped it down on the bar, and covered it with my hand. "Thirty-two dollars or the next round of drinks are free. Your call."

She smiled demurely and shook her head. "Sixteen dollars."

I gave her a twenty. She made change.

"Not much of a risk taker," I said.

"Depends," she said.

I nodded like this meant something hopeful and watched as she moved away to serve a young couple in white turtlenecks and loose-fitting suits who had seemingly drifted into the bar in time to witness our little exchange. They were a very strange pair: the woman was a petite little tease, maybe Pakistani, with a nearly transparent nylon veil drawn across her mouth and nose; and her male companion was in a wheelchair—a crew-cut corn-fed type who somehow looked Nebraskan: big and blond and beefy. He wheeled his way down the bar and slapped me on my lower back. "So how 'bout triple or nothing, Hoss? I'm real thirsty. What you say?"

I turned slightly to face him and didn't much like what I saw. On close examination his suit looked almost threadbare, but despite his massive redneck bulk, it was at least a size or two too large. His thighs were the size of saw logs—I wondered what was wrong with them. His companion's suit was almost stylish. She drummed her long pink painted nails as if she were very nervous about something. I noticed her long delicate hands.

"Sure thing. What's your poison?"

The Nebraskan looked to the veiled woman as if for advice. "Sprite," she said.

"Better let that barmaid hold your money then," I said, and pointed, and the Nebraskan began to shake his head but stopped when the barmaid gave him a wink. I didn't like that wink, but I didn't quite know what to make of it.

"Agreed," said the tiny woman, butting in. She had a middle-eastern accent that I couldn't place exactly although there was some British-school-system tempering to it. She pulled out her billfold and slid out a Platinum Visa card. I pulled out my quarter again. "Call it in the air."

"Let it fall on the floor," the big guy said. The veiled woman had moved so that they flanked me and I had one of them on either side. Very cozy. I smiled and tossed the coin.

"Heads!" the Nebraskan said.

I made sure I had a hand on my wallet, but bent to see the coin, which it had fallen between our barstools. "Tails," I said. The big guy bent over to look and nodded. When I stood up, the barmaid had already drawn my beer—it had a lot of expensive froth. "Happiness," I said. I reached out for the cup and drained it in a single gulp. I felt the tiny woman take hold of my elbow as if to steady me. I was starting to pull away from her when the bar started to spin. I tried to say something and found I couldn't speak without slurring. Then the whole room seemed to stretch and yawn and the faces got long and funny as if they were cartoons on Silly Putty, and I realized I was falling over and the big Nebraskan was standing up. Then I was sitting in his wheelchair and going somewhere I'd never been, and those cartoon colors began to fade—to gray, to charcoal, and then, quite abruptly, to black.

CHAPTER 21

I came to with a feeling of gagging and the sensation that I was about to vomit. I tried to touch my face and couldn't. My hands were bound behind my back and hogtied to my ankles with a cord that looped around my neck. A wadded pillowcase was in my mouth and over that a length of plastic coated wire had been pulled so tight I felt like the corners of my mouth were splitting. I was suffocating as I struggled so I quit and lay still and fought the urge to puke. I could breathe after a fashion but only through my nose. It was one of those times I wished I practiced yoga. Lorrie did exercises every day and was always after me to start, especially with heart disease running in my family, but I told her I'd rather get my cardiovascular workout in the sack. Now my words were coming back to haunt me and it took every bit of willpower I could muster to force myself not to struggle and just to lay still so that whatever oxygen I could suck in through my nose would be sufficient.

I closed my eyes and tried to slow my heartbeat—it wasn't easy. I was lying on a motel bed. How I'd gotten here I didn't know, but the wheelchair was stashed in a corner. I didn't see my overnight bag anywhere, but then I'd remembered I put it in an airport locker. Just a few feet away were the barmaid and the couple from the airport bar. The tiny woman wasn't wearing her veil now; in fact, she wasn't wearing anything. She and the barmaid were tangled up naked together in the second bed, and the big Nebraskan sat fully clothed in the upholstered chair. The women were making love, each with her head locked between the other's thighs and slurping happily away. That didn't bother me at all until I noticed that both women were missing their nipples—but the big Nebraskan was watching pro football on TV, and didn't pay them any mind. As a one-time porno flick director I couldn't help but admire his detachment, because on top of everything else, watching the two women go at each other gave me an immediate and ridiculous hard-on. But the big guy paid absolutely no attention until I tried to roll over and watch them. He got up and shoved me back and sat on my bed and held my head down sideways against the mattress with one of his huge pork-chop hands. The message was clear—I could watch TV but not them. He continued to watch the game. I lay there and got a sense of the room. The women were behind me now. My wallet and car keys were right there on the nightstand. My cell-phone and digital camera were in the airport locker with my coat. The blinds were drawn and the wall heater was humming away. It was a mauve-colored over-sized American motel room. Probably some national chain. The TV was loud: Chicago versus Philadelphia. I watched one running play that went nowhere, then an injury time-out that cut suddenly to a commercial for light beer while they carried a player from Philly off on a gurney. I'd never been especially interested in sports—for me, football was simply a subject for small talk with strangers. So *how about them Bears?* But I watched the game for a minute or two longer until the half-time whistle blew and a commercial for Chevy pickup trucks came on. 10 to 7. Chicago up by a field goal in the City of Brotherly Love.

"He's awake, Doc," the Nebraskan said finally. He'd been sitting there on the bed with me ever since I'd tried to move. The bed springs behind me creaked once or twice and the middle-eastern woman stood and walked through my line of vision. She was naked and nippleless, and had a shaved twat to boot, but seemed entirely nonchalant about wandering around like that. I heard a door swing open, but it was neither the door to outside nor the bathroom door so I guessed she'd entered an adjoining room. Water ran. When she came back she was carrying what looked to be a glass vial of some clear liquid and a disposable syringe. She used her teeth to tear the plastic wrapper off the syringe and drew up a measured dose. I tried to shake my head and couldn't. She looked at me with an absolutely blank expression.

"So, had enough sleep?" she asked. She had small, unbalanced, pear-shaped tits.

I tried to nod. It wasn't exactly easy with the Nebraskan's hand on my head. I could barely believe my good fortune when she bent and loosened the gag.

"Any undue noise and Mister Sandman will come again," she said.

I tried again to nod.

Nebraska unfastened the wire cord, drew out the wadded pillow—more cloth than I imagined would fit in my mouth—and I felt intensely grateful. I'd make a wonderful prisoner of war. Even a hint of torture and I'd co-operate with anyone. My throat felt as raw as a kosher butcher's knuckles. "So how about them Bears?" I said, and tried to sound bemused, but all that came out was a one-word whisper, "Bears." Even with a fuzzy head I knew that didn't make much sense.

"Get him something to drink," she said.

Nebraska got up and unwrapped a thin plastic tumbler and filled it from the bathroom sink. He held it to my lips and I sucked in some lukewarm tapwater. After swishing it around and gulping a few times, I found that I could talk again. "Fish fornicate in it," I said.

"What's that mean?" she wanted to know.

"Nothing," I said. "Old W.C. Fields line." She'd left the loaded syringe on the nightstand and I eyed it as a possible weapon. "It came up tails," I said. "You still owe me a cool one."

"Satan is strong in him," the Nebraskan said.

"Shut up, Louis," the tiny woman said.

She bent again to whisper something to me. "You had far too much to drink my friend. You fell off your bar stool."

For a second I was almost confused enough to believe her. I'd been a borderline drunk for years, and I still used whites on occasion when I needed extra energy and I smoked pot to relax, but I was very afraid of needles. I'd never injected anything because needles reminded me of doctors—and never in my worst fern-bar, happy-hour stupor had I ever been so smashed that I deserved a hangover like this. Besides, my thinking seemed pretty clear even if my vision wasn't. I decided to play for time. It was a pleasure just to breathe—a natural high, as it were. "So untie me and order some strong black coffee."

"No can do."

"We work the will of Allah," Nebraska said.

"Yes, shut up, Louis," another woman's voice said. I guessed that was the barmaid, but I couldn't see her.

"So where you folks from?" I asked. I tried to phrase the question so as to sound Bridgewater causal, like this kind of thing happened to me every other day, but under the circumstances I guessed it sounded forced.

"You would do better not to know," the middle-eastern woman said, and she bounced when she giggled, and that scared me a little, what with her nippleless tits.

"There's knowledge and there's knowing," the big Nebraskan said. There was enough reverence in his voice to let me know he was quoting from someone. "The faithful know the difference."

I watched the lady bartender smile at him.

"So what's with the catechism—he the idiot savant or what?"

"Louis is a bit of a zealot, but we rely on him to keep us spiritually centered," the barmaid said. She was leaning over me now.

"You lost me," I said.

"You who are lost to Allah are lost to salvation," Louis said. He looked proud of himself.

"Lost isn't the word," I said. "Why not untie me?"

"You will be released in good time."

"Our Jihad is the god-head made flesh," Louis said. "Ours is the third advent."

"No shit," I said. "Tell me more."

"Shut up, Louis," the tiny woman said.

"So how do I join the faithful?" I asked him. "I think I've seen the light."

Louis suddenly looked very angry.

"He uses words as a rapier, Louis," the barmaid cautioned. "He's an infidel—don't let him provoke you."

"Yeah, don't take it personally, Louis," I said. "It's not your fault you're deluded and pussy-whipped. Blame it on your low IQ."

The woman smiled. "Louis would snap your neck—I'd have only to ask him."

"Now why would you want to do something like that?"

She seemed surprised by the question. "Allah has seen fit to bless our joining. Louis is my husband."

"Mazel tov," I said.

She frowned. "You don't understand. Procreation is forbidden us. You see how we have marked ourselves." She touched her nippleless breasts.

"Protecting the gene pool?"

"Procreative sex is banned," she said matter-of-factly. "We choose to be so marked. But with Allah's permission some are allowed to sublimate. It's—what's the American word—a perk for martyrs and cadre leaders."

I decided to let that wash. "If you wanted to kill me, I'd already be dead. I saw what you did to Greenwood."

She didn't even blink at that. "We wish you to cease your investigations into the death of Jasper McLean."

"Absolutely," I said. "Scout's honor."

"I like to take a man at his word," she said.

"So untie me."

She picked up the syringe instead. "You were planning to return to Bridgewater" she said, and drove the silvery needle home.

When I came to again, I knew hours had passed. I had pissed the bed, my ass was sore, and my legs were cold and clammy, but my prick and balls were still present and accounted for, and I was again tied up like a bullcalf, and once again I was gagged. I could probably roll off the bed and maybe worm my way to the outside door and bang on it with my head until somebody noticed, but I was wasn't sure I'd make it there without hanging myself on the cord around my neck. The TV was turned up loud but was coming from the other room now. I listened closely. Football again, but a new game with different teams. I wondered vaguely if the Bears had won.

I wormed myself towards the nightstand with the room phone and my keys and wallet—which looked like it had been fingered through but still had money in it. If could get the receiver off the hook and dial 911, I could probably summon help. I used my chin to push the receiver off its cradle. It made a clatter as it dropped onto the nightstand but nobody rushed in from the connecting room. I listened for a dial tone—it was there. Then I tried to dial, and was far less successful. My chin was too large and my nose too soft to push one button at a time. I had to keep hanging up and trying to dial again and again. Every time I bobbed my head the cord cut into my throat. It was so damn frustrating I started wondering if I should simply lie back and die and save everybody the trouble of killing me, but finally I managed it. I made some noise, not much, some banging and some grunts, and that I was all I had left. I heard the operator get frantic and hoped they would trace the call. Then I lay back quietly, and for a while I heard nothing.

I was probably out for a good while, but I more or less came to consciousness when somebody finally pounded on the door and yelled, "Open up! Police!"

For once, such words were a welcome sound, but I couldn't respond. I tried to shake off the drug but my eyelids felt glued in place, and when I wiggled my neck the rope cut off my breathing. *Sorry. All tied up at the moment.* A minute later, when I finally got my eyes open, four cops were in the room, sweeping through with walkie-talkies squawking on their belts. Probably the desk had given them a passkey.

One of the cops untied me, and I coughed when he pulled out the gag.

He stared at me. "You wanna tell us what this is all about?"

"Ah, Sergeant, maybe we'd better ask him questions later," another of the cops said. He'd been listening to his walkie-talkie. We got ourselves a bomb threat. Somebody called it in."

The one who'd been talking to me bent and took a very quick look under the bed. What he saw there I didn't know, but his face went pale. "Let's go," he said. "Everybody out! Evacuate!"

He finished untying my knots. "Can you walk, buddy?"

I staggered to my feet. Things were happening a little fast. I grabbed my wallet and car keys from the nightstand, stuck my feet into shoes without bothering with the laces. He helped me lurch into the hall. By then I was feeling a little bit better and was able to followed him down a flight of concrete fire stairs and outside under my own power. It was dark out and cold—which surprised me more than a little because I'd lost track of time. I learned I'd been staying at a Ramada Inn by the airport. I could see huge planes approaching for landing, passing right over the parking lot.

He pressed down on my head so as to sit me down in the back seat of the patrol car and was about to close the door when I finally began to puke. My long loose hair was flying around my face. The cop left the door open so I wouldn't stink up his car and watched me double up and groan. Finally, he called for medical backup on the radio. Listening, I learned that a bomb disposal squad had been dispatched. I heard a fire alarm inside the building start to sound, and it howled and didn't stop. In what seemed like less than a minute a hundred or more people were milling around the lot in their pajamas and bathrobes: tourists, newlyweds, and entire families with sleepy kids wrapped up in blankets and hotel bedspreads.

Next the fire department arrived, three trucks with revolving lights and firemen in rubber boots. The cop had opened up his trunk and was fishing around for some yellow crime scene tape. He had the roll in his hand when we heard the explosion—a huge dusty blast that took out a second-story window and filled the night with orange flames and yellow sparks as if from a giant magnesium flare. I put my head down and puked again. The blast had simultaneously extinguished every light in the hotel including the neon sign.

"Holy shit," the cop said, but looked away when he saw me retching. "Sit tight," he said," and started towards the burning building, leaving me momentarily unattended. I waited a long minute, considering my options. Then I staggered to my feet and started toward the airport. Behind me were the fireworks and chaos, but ahead I could see planes kept taking off and coming in for landings—as if nothing were out of the ordinary That obviously wouldn't last. I walked for about a quarter mile, ran a hundred yards or so, quit because my stomach hurt, and walked along wheezing and spitting and holding my side for a while before I tried to run again.

But in less than ten minutes I was back inside the baggage claim where I limped to a rest room to clean myself as best I could and raked my fingers through my hair and stood studying my face in a metal mirror. I looked like early death and sooner or later they'd probably catch me, but maybe not. There wasn't much of anything left to identify me. My fingerprints were on file in any number of places, but after a fire like that, in a motel room that had probably been occupied by thousands of straying fingers, the furniture blown all to hell and pissed on by the sprinkler system—well, an investigation wouldn't yield anything but ashes and confusion. Even if by some remote chance there were still some prints left, it would take them weeks or months to sort anything out. I couldn't remember touching anything in that patrol car.

I'd obviously lost more than twelve hours and I'd missed my flight and damaged a few essential brain cells, and my expensive first-class ticket was no longer inside my wallet, but for inexplicable reasons—perhaps some strange theological ones—those sexy Islamic lesbians hadn't bothered to take my cash. Dirty money left to burn, I suppose. Similarly, although it looked as if they'd fingered though my various licenses and maxed-out credit-cards, all six fake IDs were rather amazingly still there.

CHAPTER *22*

On the sidewalk outside the baggage claim I managed to hail a
yellow cab, and in minutes I was moving forward again. I directed
the cab driver to take me to the nearest liquor store and to wait
while I purchased a bottle of Southern Comfort to counteract all the
drugs and adrenaline in my system, kill my bad breath, and help me
think. The first drink went down easy so I had another, and another.
I tried closing my eyes and meditating but I kept visualizing burnt
bodies with nasty holes in them. Gunshot wounds and stab wounds
and white bloodless flesh that closed over apertures like a puckered
mouth.

I knew, of course, that I probably ought to eat something, so as
not to start a drinking binge on an empty stomach, but I all could
imagine my overtaxed system tolerating was some honey-roasted
peanuts, dry soda crackers, or maybe a tiny fruit cocktail in a plastic
cup with tiny cubes of peaches and pears and maraschino cherry
halves floating around like weightless astronauts in heavy syrup.
Outer-space food. Divorced from the earth and all things carnal.

But I obviously couldn't drift off gently into orbit just yet, so I
had another drink and told the taxi driver to circle downtown Philly
until I decided where I wanted to go. Every five minutes I had
another shot of whiskey, and I started staring though the back
window of the cab as if I were watching the world though a port-
hole. I couldn't tell where I was exactly but I was soon so loaded

it didn't matter. I could close my eyes or open them and the images rolled on.

By now it was raining, and the cab driver, a moon-faced black guy, who sort of reminded me of Fats Domino, although he really looked nothing like him, was checking me out almost constantly in his rear view. "Are you tight, man?" he kept asking.

"Women problems," I told him, which seemed to satisfy his curiosity, at least temporarily. But I was disgusted with myself. Not only did I look bad and smell bad, but I'd cracked the rear window to keep my stench from offending the cabby, and the cold air had made my neck knot up. My ears hurt too, and my nose had started to drip. Simply because I had a half-ass excuse, I'd already made a pig of myself and guzzled down so much booze that my stomach had turned sour and I'd slid into a hangover without even bothering to get high. I was in a nasty, suicidal funk, and I had to keep telling myself my luck had been remarkable simply to keep thinking about ways to stay alive rather than slow ways I could off myself. I felt sick and entrapped by my own flesh, and I couldn't help but wonder if this kind of feeling wasn't what Jasper McLean must have experienced those last groggy moments in his car.

I counted the things I had to be thankful for. I counted them on my fingers. I hadn't been perforated by specialty bullets. I hadn't been cut to sticky red shreds back in the airport john in Bridgewater. Those religious nuts hadn't OD'd me on whatever crap it was they'd sedated me with. I'd gotten out of a Ramada Inn without paying for the room. I still had cash in my wallet along with multiple IDs. I hadn't been suffocated or blown up or burned to death. A kind cop had gotten sloppy and hadn't even asked my name—which meant I wasn't technically a fugitive—yet. Sooner or later they might figure out who I was and place me at the hotel explosion, but there wasn't enough evidence to charge me with anything so long as I kept my mouth shut.

It was only a about two days ago that I'd first met Mrs. McLean. It seemed like a lot longer. I hadn't made it to Florida, and I'd neglected to send Bosco and Geno an alligator postcard, but they'd have to forgive me—I'd had other things on my mind.

For the moment, flying away to anywhere else was probably out of the question, but I could find a cheap hotel in here in Philly and simply sleep things off—or I could rent myself a car and head back to Bridgewater. The more I thought about a rental car, the better I liked the idea. I wanted to get a jump on things. In another eight hard hours or so I could be back home in Bridgewater—probably in time to watch the sun rise over the sewage-enriched waters of Long Island Sound. Maybe I'd go see Lorrie and sack out in her apartment. O *were I in my lover's arms and in her bed again.*

I sincerely doubted that anybody had permanently staked out Bridgewater Airport to make sure I didn't return, but I'd somehow already offended Sal Almonde's psychotic underlings and the nutty Islamic threesome enough to make all of them willing—perhaps even eager—to kill me, and I was still clueless as to why. Bosco and Geno had obviously alerted the Islamic folk and told them to track me though the Philadelphia airport until I got on the Florida flight. And maybe they would have had had someone waiting for me at that Florida airport too.

It certainly seemed like Almonde's people were going through significant effort and expense to keep me away from Bridgewater. Had this madness been precipitated by my taking on the McLean case? And where did the nippleless lesbians figure in? The trouble was they didn't. It simply seemed like there were crazy people after my ass everywhere, and no place was really safe until I found out what I'd done wrong. Even then I wouldn't be safe—but at least I'd be better informed. Anyway, since only Geno and Bosco had known that I'd be connecting through Philly—and so probably also knew by now that I wasn't in Florida, and also knew exactly where I'd parked in Bridgewater Municipal, then they'd surely know that I'd returned if my Escort somehow got moved.

A rental car could be perfect—if I got the right one. I wanted to avoid the major car companies because they were all highly computerized, and if the cops had connections to trace credit card files, Sal Almonde's people probably had such connections as well. What better way to trace people who owed you money than to know exactly where they were using plastic? That left renting a car for cash and that certainly put a crimp in things. I had two possible options—Lease-a-Lemon or Rent-a-Wreck. Both were regional rental companies and served a kind of clientele that didn't have much credit-worthiness, but both would rent you a car for cash if you put down a hefty deposit.

My cab driver looked very relieved when I finally told where I wanted to go, and I paid him fifty-five dollars, which included a decent tip.

CHAPTER 23

The fat guy behind the Rent-a-Wreck counter wanted an eight-hundred-dollar rental deposit on a vehicle that rented for $29.95 a day with unlimited mileage. He was a large man with a pencil thin mustache. He examined my bogus New Jersey driver's license: Philip Larkin.

"Eight hundred dollars? What's that, book value of the car?" I asked him.

"Right-o," he said.

"We're trying to discourage cash rentals."

I almost told him to go fuck himself, but I needed a vehicle badly enough to give him the money for the car and another eighty dollars for the full coverage insurance—which I figured was prudent—and he gave me the keys.

"It's a Pontiac," he said and smiled. "Nine years old, and eight cylinders but she runs like a gazelle." He was trying hard to be a colorful character.

"Probably gets lousy mileage," I said. I wasn't in the mood for colorful characters.

This reminded him of something. "You gotta return it full," he said, or we fill it and charge you."

"Yeah, yeah, yeah," I said and went out into the rain. In the lot I unlocked the car and started the engine. The interior smelled of cheap cigarettes. The driver's armrest was loose. The windshield had a chip in it. The hubcaps were mismatched. But the tires looked new and a big V-8 purred smoothly under the hood. It pleased me. Except for out-of-state tags it was exactly the kind of car that would blend perfectly in downtown Bridgewater, a place I was going back to because it seemed like the wrong thing to do. Yin and Yang. Pick one from column A and one from column B. You pays your money and you orders the double cheeseburger. Besides, if I wasn't safe in Bridgewater I probably wasn't safe anywhere, and I'd just as soon be somewhere where I had a girlfriend and a father to blame for my unhappiness. I pulled out of the lot and was halfway down the block when I realized the gas tank was only three quarters full and considered going back, but I kept on driving.

It was rain all the way back to Connecticut. Slow going. Especially around the tolls where traffic had backed up. A cold raw night and I drove cautiously in the rented Pontiac, blinded by headlights of tractor trailers and greasy road spray that smeared things. The Pontiac felt huge after my Escort, and despite the good tires, it seemed to be hydroplaning. Besides, I wasn't yet completely sober. My eyes hurt, my head hurt, and my stomach kept doing flip flops. In novels, detectives were made of far sturdier stuff. They got socked in the jaw or hit with an empty bottle or shot full of drugs and simply kept moving forward.

I wanted to lie down and rest now. I might even be able to sleep at a rest area, but I wasn't feeling particularly healthy today. All I'd really survived so far was a plane trip or two, a sedated day in bed, a bombing, a car rental, and a hangover, but somewhere around South Norwalk I passed a three-car pile-up and suddenly interstate traffic seemed too much to handle. I took an exit for the Post Road where I hoped to find a place to eat and drink coffee. I needed to quiet my nerves, but I didn't see any place open until I'd driven past a couple of diners.

Finally, I saw a familiar blinking vacancy sign for a motel called the Starburst where the night clerk wouldn't charge sales tax if you paid in cash. I knew about the Starburst because they also had hourly rates and occasionally I'd visit the pickup bars in Westport or Fairfield and get lucky with some dumb, drunk college girl from Fairfield University or Sacred Heart. We'd use a room for an hour or so—sometimes less—and then leave. According to Lorrie, such behavior had its roots in a general hostility toward women and likely stemmed from the fact that my mother had also abandoned me when she left my father. I hadn't seen my mother since, so I figured there was something to that, but I had only vague warm memories of her, a small blunt-featured woman who had cried often and softly and who liked to rock me in her arms long after I was too old for that. I had a photograph or two of her and me taken back when I was an infant, but my father had always refused to talk much about their marriage, and exactly what this had to do with picking up willing coeds in bars I wasn't sure, but Lorrie seemed certain I had some deep psychological wound, and I didn't want to argue because I sensed that her believing this helped keep her broadminded and tolerant about what I persisted in thinking of as my infidelities—although she had insisted she would never try to limit me in that way.

Anyway, I chose to forget about having coffee and instead turned into the Starburst where I gave a sleepy night clerk four twenty dollar bills and told him I needed a wake-up call at seven. It was two in the morning. He told me I could set the alarm clock in the room. I told him I didn't want to mess with it. He told me okay. I'd signed the motel register as Mr. Jonathan Edwards.

The sound of the ringing phone woke me. Sunlight was streaming in because I hadn't bothered to close the heavy drapes completely. I winced and grunted into the mouthpiece.

"Eight o'clock sharp, Mr. Edwards." It was a teenager's voice. She sounded cheerful.

"Forgiveness is harder to come by than remorse," I said.

"Pardon me?" she said. She sounded a little flustered. "Anyway it's eight."

"Thanks," I said. "I needed that."

As soon as I had showered, I left the room key on the TV for the chambermaid to find when I left. I didn't really want to put my same smelly clothes back on but didn't have any choice. Then I sat quietly for a while in my moldy old rental car, letting the engine warm as I counted the remaining cash in my wallet. Six hundred eighty dollars of the original thirty-five hundred. That the wallet hadn't been emptied by the religious freaks still amazed me. Robbery obviously wasn't their thing, but I'd known that all along. Where did their rogue brand of Islamic fundamentalism fit into all this? What might they have against me that would merit felony kidnapping and their destruction of a Ramada Inn? I didn't know and didn't care—I wasn't so crazy about the Ramada Inn anyway. In a forty-eight-hour period I'd already burned though nearly all of Mrs. McLean's advance, and I felt rather guilty and a little sad about that, but not enough to risk calling Mrs. McLean and revealing my whereabouts. For all I knew, Sal Almonde had tapped her phone. Paranoid? Probably. But if Almonde discovered I was back in town after being warned off, I'd be hamburger meat.

I headed down the road toward Bridgewater, pulled into the drive-in lane at McDonald's, and ordered a Big Breakfast with orange juice and coffee to go because I'd decided not to chance being recognized. Sipping a large black coffee that tasted of sweet Styrofoam, I rolled along. I found a 7-Eleven store and bought a full tank of off-brand gas and a toothbrush and a pair of dark wrap-around sunglasses, and when I looked in the mirror, the effect was weird but not unpleasant. I looked and felt like a stranger—and for a half second or so I honestly didn't know who I was. I felt lost, and maybe lonely, but not especially afraid, and that absence of fear cued me into realizing that I'd better backtrack immediately and seek some professional help.

It suddenly seemed so likely I'd be dead by tomorrow that I found myself wondering if maybe I didn't really exist, like maybe I'd never existed, like my life hadn't and didn't matter—which it hadn't and didn't, and moreover was beside the point. Besides, I already missed Lorrie and had deep questions to ask her. Why, for instance, was I still going through the motions and acting like a responsible private detective when I'd already more or less decided to pocket Mrs. McLean's money and shut down shop. Was I becoming actively self-destructive or what? Why had I headed back to Bridgewater of all places? Maybe I'd thought I was being brave and noble, but perhaps my returning was an act of surrender? Had I given up caring if I lived or died? Shouldn't I be operating in some sort of survival mode? Wasn't the compulsion to ask these inane questions a sure sign that I suffered from some deep-seated sickness, some strange free-floating guilt? Yes, I missed Lorrie. I was even starting to think like her. I sometimes wondered if one of the reasons I saw Lorrie Moore and had frequently asked her to marry me wasn't because she helped me to compartmentalize my own madness. After my fifty-minute therapy sessions we would usually be so worn out and so ready to jump one another's bones that for a while after our lovemaking I'd usually feel okay and could repress my own propensity to over-analyze things and get on with my sorry life.

I called Lorrie from an open-air pay phone in the corner of the 7-Eleven parking lot. Traveling without a cell phone, I'd sort of gotten into the habit of looking for phone booths. The passing traffic was so loud that I kept one ear pressed tightly against the phone's receiver and stuck a finger in my other ear like the muzzle of a gun while I punched in her number. I got her prune-faced receptionist on the line.

"Ms. Moore, please."

"Ms. Moore is with a client."

"This is Mr. Khan."

"May I have her call you back, Mr. Khan?"

"Just tell her it's important."

"Is there a number where she can reach you."

"I'll hold."

"She may be in session for a while yet."

"Tell her it's urgent."

"Just as soon as she's done, Sir."

A gasoline tanker truck had pulled up beside the phone and parked. I breathed in a deep lungful of the diesel exhaust fumes and listened to the engine idle. Jasper McLean had gotten off easy. At least he got to die at home in his own garage.

"Better interrupt," I said, "I need to speak to Lorrie now." I paused.

"Tell her it's life and death!"

"Please hold," she said, and sounded disgusted.

There was a click and then some old folk music to listen to, but the volume was so low it was almost inaudible. It took me a while to identify exactly what I was listening to. It was "Blowing in the Wind" as sung by Odetta, who'd actually died not all that long ago, so maybe it was some kind of tribute, but to me it seemed like such a song had been intentionally selected by somebody as to make the hangers-on feel hopeless and hang up.

I waited another long minute.

"Peter?" Lorrie said, finally.

"Hey, Princess," I said. "Real good to hear your voice again."

"Peter," she said. "Don't be hostile."

I considered this. I knew Lorrie disliked it when I called her "Princess." It was short for Afro-American princess and a standing joke between us.

"Peter, is anything really wrong?"

"Life and death," I said, "Mostly death." Then I laughed with what I certainly hoped sounded like irony and not hysteria. "Same old, same old shit."

"Peter, I was with a very distraught client. I had to end the session early."

"Sal Almonde?"

"Why do you ask?"

"Damnit," I said. "The fucker's trying to kill me."

"Peter," Lorrie said. "Could this be paranoia?"

"Yeah," I said. "Strange voices in my head."

"Well," Lorrie said. "If you must know, I was with a very depressed young housewife."

I watched the driver get out of the cab and use a metal pry to remove a cover so he could access the storage tanks. I watched him drag a thick white rubber hose from the coil on his truck and ease the hose end down into the access shaft.

"Fuck me, Lorrie," I said. "I've met some very troubled folks in the last twenty-four hours who are not very depressed young housewives. I think Almonde's somehow connected."

"Peter, you know how you get."

"Lorrie, I'm not being paranoid!"

"Peter, is there something else that's gone wrong?"

I watched the truck driver turn a valve that started a squealing pump and let gasoline flow through his hose. I could barely hear what Lorrie was saying over the sound of his pump and had already almost forgotten why I'd called her. I pressed my trigger finger a little deeper into my one free ear.

"Listen, can you make some time for me this afternoon? I really need to talk at length with someone sane."

Lorrie asked me to hold again while she checked her appointment book. I heard the very last notes of "Blowing in the Wind" and then nearly all of "Wichita Lineman" before Lorrie picked up the phone again.

"Peter, I'm booked solid. But we could we talk on the phone for a few minutes if you'd like?"

It wasn't what I wanted, but I guessed it would have to do. The truck's driver had finished pumping.

"Lorrie, what makes a person want to join a religious cult?"

"Peter, is that what you called about?" She sounded angry, and that really pissed me off.

"What kind of asshole do you take me for?"

There was a long pause. "You leave yourself wide open Peter," she said, and I realized that she was pretty pissed off herself. I felt oddly empowered. Talking to a loving therapist had helped me after all.

"Want to get together after work?" I asked her.

"I've got my aerobics class," she said. "I'm supposed to be leading the group tonight while our instructor's on vacation."

"That's why I love you, Princess," I said. "You're always there."

"You're not being entirely fair or even clear, Peter."

"Now, now," I said. "I'm aware that a beautiful body requires upkeep."

"Frankly, I think that's a very sexist remark."

"Not simply sexist," I said. "Only sort of semi-sexist. And you do have a beautiful body—you're just insecure about it."

"I've really got to get off," Lorrie said. "You can call me late, after aerobics if you like."

"I'll let you go," I said, and hung up.

The tanker truck was just pulling away, and it belched a final cloud of black exhaust in my face as it left the lot.

CHAPTER 24

My next stop was the downtown Salvation Army store where I bought myself an assortment of better smelling clothes—mostly button-down dress shirts and tan chinos, all of which seemed reasonably clean but didn't fit me very well. I told myself that it was just some stuff to keep me going. I used their dressing room to change.

I also made plans to visit the Bridgewater Public Library—always one of my favorite haunts—where I had the usual difficulty finding a place to park. Lately, the city was so insolvent that they'd cut back the library's open hours to seventeen per week, and no matter when I'd tried to use it over the last year I'd usually found the glass doors bolted and the building dark. An often-closed public library seemed a symbol for something I couldn't quite put my finger on—unless it was, as Lorrie had once suggested, a symbol for the possibility of rejection from a safe human community I could willingly be part of, and, consequently, a metaphor for my fear of a socially integrated self. Again, I didn't quite believe this, but I couldn't think of anything that sounded better, and, on some level, I supposed she was right.

The strange thing was that an often-closed public library also seemed like part of a larger impersonal pattern. In an American culture that made a virtue out of greed, was it really any wonder that "socialism" was a dirty word?

It wasn't that I had any illusions about socialism as a system, which had never really worked anywhere, not even in McLean's depression-era Bridgewater, but for some reason I still clung to the dream that one day people might find some way to share with one another and that simple self-interest didn't *always* need to be the controlling principle.

Fortunately, the library was open today and the person at the information desk was a cross-eyed peroxide blond in a short leather miniskirt that showcased her blotchy thighs. She'd been sitting on the desk with one plump leg crossed over the other and swinging provocatively. On her feet were crepe-soled sandals with red leather thongs that had already rubbed the skin raw between her crooked toes.

"I wonder if you could help me, Miss," I said.

"I'm on break," she said and snapped pink gum when she spoke. She didn't sound like any librarian I'd ever known, and I suspected I'd seen her once or twice flagging cars outside the post office on Water Street.

"Yeah," I said. "Well, maybe you could help me anyway. It might be worth considering." I put the emphasis on "worth."

That got her attention. "Maybe," she said, eying me suspiciously. "What's your need?"

"I need some help with the microfilm machine."

"Fuck off."

"Then how about a little professional tenderness?"

"Like I told you," she said. "I'm on break." She stared at her chewed fingernails, endeavoring to look bored.

"One time for love?" I said.

She gave me a look of absolute disbelief. Like she'd just been propositioned by a guy who bought his clothes from secondhand stores and hung around the public library.

"One hundred dollars," I whispered. "Five minutes of your time."

That got her moving. She stood up and I followed her to the elevator. We got in and she pushed the button. We rose and I rose, almost despite myself. But what the fuck had compelled me to offer her a hundred dollars?

"You don't seem much like a librarian," I said, simply to be saying something. We were staring at each other like rats in a window box.

"I'm Job Corps," she said. "My parole officer got me this library to train in." She pronounced it "lie-berry."

"Good honest work," I said because by then I knew with absolute certainty exactly what she'd been arrested for.

"So you the man?" she asked suddenly. "If I ask you if you the man, you got to tell me if you the man, right?"

"Right," I said, because honestly wasn't required. "I'm definitely not the man."

"For a hundred dollars," she said. "I'll do you fine." She wiggled her fat posterior and wet her lips.

"No problem," I said. "But only if you show me how to thread the microfilm first."

"You serious?"

"Does the man talk shit?"

"Kinky, kinky," she said and laughed. "Everybody's complicated." The elevator stopped and opened, and she led me to the machines, flicked a switch so that a light bulb lit and the screen began to hum; then she grabbed an available canister and threaded film so fast I could barely follow her. "Just do it like this," she said.

"Great," I said, thoroughly shocked that she actually knew how something worked, but when I sat down at the machine she seemed so terribly disappointed that I pulled out my wallet and gave her four twenties and two tens. I had less than three-hundred dollars left.

She seemed genuinely surprised but pocketed the money, and when I turned to the machine again she shook her head and said, "You must be crazy."

"Not entirely," I said. "I interrupted your break."

She touched my shoulder. "Well, come on then," she said.

"Look," I said, "it's not really necessary."

"Follow me."

I got up and she led me to a tiny typing carrel. The door was wire-webbed glass, but it was mostly masked by a cardboard poster advertising a community art exhibit that had come and gone a month ago. She pushed the typewriter aside so I could recline on the desk.

"You really don't owe me anything," I said, but didn't mean it, because, of course, some part of me wanted to get whatever extra I could for my hard-earned hundred bucks.

She just smiled. "One time for love," she said.

So I sat on the desk and she unzipped me, slipped a latex skin on my erection, and took my flesh in her mouth so quickly and professionally that I barely had time to gasp. I didn't bother to hold back. She sucked, I came, and when I did she looked at me and smiled her cross-eyed smile.

I sighed with something that wasn't contentment as she carefully removed the skin and tied it off while I zipped myself up again. She tossed the condom into a metal trash can, and on the way back to the microforms she didn't say a word, but when we passed a water fountain, I watched her bend and swish and spit.

I gave her a little wave as she walked on by. I didn't turn around to look, but I heard the elevator start down and suddenly felt it necessary to lose myself in my work.

The research took hours. I started with Jasper McLean's death because I knew the date, fast-forwarded a week to glean the depress ing details about his funeral—mostly names I didn't recognize, then started working my way back through the front pages of the local paper—the *Daily Telegram* back then—looking for some political decision that involved a large amount of money. It was hard to keep focused and stay sharp when I didn't know what I was looking for. There was the tendency to drift or else to get caught up in some old story that had nothing to do with anything. The hardest thing in the world was to work alone, to seek some unknown thing blindly with no certainty of success. The tendency was to doubt, to dismiss your intuitions, to let your thoughts meander until trying to concentrate seemed foolish and impossible. The hard thing was to go at it methodically, to make sure you didn't miss something, knowing all the while that you wouldn't know if you did.

Fortunately, I was only on task for about two hours before I came across an article written about three weeks before McLean's death.

What I'd found was only a few lines of news copy in a summary of the decisions made at a weekly city council meeting, but I felt the dark hairs on my arms prickle.

Representing the city as the majority stockholder of the Bridgewater Land Corporation, Mayor McLean had agreed to re-lease a right-of-way owned by Bridgewater Land to the New York-Connecticut Railroad—for fifty years, beginning in 1960—for one dollar a year. But in exchange for leasing the right-of-way, Mayor McLean had negotiated concessions from the New York-Connecticut that linked tonnage fees for local industry and ticket prices for Bridgewater commuters to gross New York-Connecticut profits.

It didn't even seem like a particularly good deal for the city unless maybe you were the kind of person who thought hard about balancing the economic impact of such decisions on something other than your own financial interests or even the temporary interest of the city you represented. It was a "big picture" way of looking at a system as important enough to be structured for the long-term economic benefit of everybody involved. Could Jasper McLean have been that kind of man?

I dug around in my pockets until I came up with a tarnished quarter and photocopied the page. Then I looked over my shoulder and turned off the machine and unthreaded the microfilm. This was as good a place to start as any, and staring at the microfilm reader had made me a little drowsy.

Unless my math was bad, a fifty year lease that began in 1960 would be up for renewal this year. I had an intuitive notion I'd lucked onto something, but I needed to do some additional research to be sure. I needed to look at a tax map and discover exactly who owned what. And I needed to investigate the Bridgewater Land Corporation. Maybe I could even figure out why McLean had decided to structure the lease the way he had, because, unless I had it wrong, that decision had gotten him dead.

CHAPTER *25*

According to John Donne, no man is an island. No woman either. But loneliness makes the world spin because some of us are peninsulas and some are mercury-poisoned rivers and some are uncharted coral reefs. And some of us are lawn chairs and some are dirty ashtrays, and a few, like Lorrie, are chocolate ice-cream sandwiches.

There isn't any way for love to save the world. It's already too far gone. Nonetheless, there's still such a thing as friendship and every so often you have to ask somebody to help. Unfortunately, I'd never had many friends, except, of course, for Lorrie, and our relationship had been complicated by therapy and sex.

Fortunately, I did have some close acquaintances, and any number of people I'd worked for or with, people who wouldn't deliberately fuck me over because I'd never fucked them over, and, consequently, could be called on. I found a pay phone by the library's entrance.

The first name on my list was Carlos Wayne, an old-time insurance man who had handled my father's "estate planning" after my parents' divorce. Thirty years ago he'd been a dandy, a smooth-talking well-closeted homosexual who'd become less and less well-closeted as the years went on. Nowadays, my father would never have bought an insurance policy from him, but nowadays he didn't sell much insurance, functioning instead as a portfolio manager—

an investment counselor, he called himself. He was the closest thing I had to a buddy who might know something useful about business.

I dialed his number and got a secretary who put me through when I lied and told her I was calling long distance—from Florida.

"Carlos," I said, "I need a favor. I'll pay whatever's fair."

"Peter, I haven't heard your lovely voice in ages. How's your old man?"

"Fine," I said. "But listen, I need your help."

"As does the entire pathetically macho world, my boy."

"Carlos, I need some detailed financial information about a real-estate company, Bridgewater Land. I need to know what it owns and the names of the owners. But the inquiry has to be discreet. It could get somebody killed."

Carlos whistled softly into the phone. "Not easy," he said. "Discretion's certainly my specialty, but if the stock isn't traded, such information's probably limited. Privately held corporations aren't closely regulated. There's very little required paperwork they're required to file—not even a quarterly report so long as they pay taxes. It mainly depends on when and where they incorporated. If it's a relatively new company they may never even have had to explain what kind of business they're in. Blue sky laws—courtesy of Ronald Reagan."

"This would be an old, old company. Half a century old anyway. And one of the things they own is a railroad line in Bridgewater. And the City of Bridgewater is the majority stockholder, so there's got to be some public records."

"Maybe right here in Connecticut then, but probably Delaware," Carlos said, "or maybe an old Pennsylvanian incorporation. I'll tiptoe through the on-line data—see what turns up. You might get lucky and there'll be an incorporation charter. I can't promise you the moon."

"Thanks, Carlos," I said. "Just make absolutely certain your inquiries can't be traced."

"Sounds serious."

"Well," I said, "it might be."

"Where can I reach you?"

"I'll call tomorrow," I said. "I'm vacationing in Florida."

"Stay out of that nasty tropic sun," Carlos said. "They say it gives you cancer."

"I'll remember," I said.

"Do say hello to your old man."

"Will do," I said, but hung up and immediately forgot.

I might have taken time for lunch, but I was on a downward roll. I headed straight for City Hall, into the rancid belly of the beast. I was looking for some forty-odd-year-old political records. I didn't know where else to start. Before leaving the library for good, I'd stopped at the information desk again and asked the Job Corps girl about how to find old city documents. She told me they didn't store them and that I should try City Hall and basically pretended she didn't know me—which she didn't—but that bothered me for some reason, after our little exchange.

At City Hall I found the city record office in the basement of a windowless room that smelled like a Xerox machine. Behind the counter was a pregnant woman, very dark-skinned and somehow tropical looking with huge gold hoop earrings and her hair done up in rows of beads. She was reading a paperback copy of Joseph Conrad's *Heart of Darkness.*

"Help you?"

"Yes, Ma'am," I said. "I'm sure you don't get many requests like this, but you see I'm a writer. I'm writing a big historical novel about the boom times of Bridgewater. It's set in the late 1950s and I'd like to look at some old political records," I hesitated, "for atmosphere."

She put down her book. "A writer, huh? What kind of atmosphere you be interested in?"

"Real estate transactions, city council meeting minutes, that kind of thing."

"From the late 1950s?"

"Right."

"You know, you the second request for real estate records from the 1950s this week."

I fought to keep my voice calm. This was almost too easy. "Is that so?"

"The mayor his-self wanted to look at that stuff."

"No shit," I said.

"But I told him we don't have it any longer," she said.

"Yeah," I said. "But I think you meant to say *no mo'*."

"Say what?"

"You said, `we don't have it *any longer.* I think you meant to say 'we don't have it *no mo'*.'"

She smiled warily. "Well, it's not easy to maintain one's bi-dialectical consistency. One may occasionally slip up."

I shook my head. "Right," I said. "So you told the mayor that you didn't know anything?"

"Can't say," she said, "and actually, that was before I consulted with my mom. She held this job nearly twenty years before she passed it on to me." She hesitated. "It's not a job you keep if you know things."

"Mom ever tell you to beware of fumes from copier machines?"

She frowned. "Listen, it's twelve bucks an hour and city insurance. Full medical and dental plan." She patted her child-swollen belly as if to soothe some slight disturbance. "I won't be here forever."

"About those records?"

"Man, they've got mountains of old records in boxes at the Bailey Museum that nobody ever looked at."

"So the mayor got what he wanted after all?"

"How I know?" she said. "He be wantin' me to run over there and fetch stuff back fo' him. As if I be some slave-girl got to run his silly errands." She smiled again. "How's that?"

"You'd fool some of the people some of the time," I said. "So it's all there at the Bailey Museum?"

"All manner stuff in boxes over dere."

"I'll look," I said. Then I hesitated. "Thanks."

She nodded. "So what's the real skinny?"

"It's one of the things you don't want to know about."

"So I can maintain plausible deniability, you mean?"

I nodded. "By the way," I said. "You wouldn't have an old tax map

I could have?"

"From the '50s? The mayor wanted one of those too."

"A current map would be fine."

"Thirty-three dollars," she said, and took one from beneath the counter. "Contractors want them all the time."

I opened my thinning wallet and gave her a fifty. She made change. "One last question." I said. "How do you like the novel?"

"Mr. Conrad, he dead," she said and beamed a smile at me that showed me her dental-plan teeth.

The Bailey Museum was an architectural anomaly in downtown Bridgewater, an ornate, five-story, Victorian brownstone complete with castle-like turrets, leaded-glass windows, and an onion-dome roof of weathered green copper. The odd thing was the building wasn't really all that old. It had been designed during Jasper McLean's administration, when Mr. J. A. Bailey, the entertainment tycoon of Barnum and Bailey fame, had temporarily "adopted" the city. After his retirement from the circus business, he'd made it his winter headquarters. Sparing absolutely no expense, Mr. Bailey had built and actually lived in the big brownstone for decades before he'd been forced by McLean to deed it to the city in lieu of paying back-owed property taxes.

For a time, it had housed assorted Bailey memorabilia: personal effects, private letters, and leftovers from his Greatest-Show-on-Earth days—midget costumes, a stuffed elephant, a moth-eaten Egyptian mummy—all of it jumbled together with old office furniture and obsolete tax records. Then, back in 1976, the city got some federal money to prepare for the upcoming bicentennial and used it to renovate the bottom four floors, then turned the building into a museum of sorts. The top floor was still a jumble, dark and musty with piles of cardboard boxes filled with paperwork molding away under blue plastic tarps. I learned all this from a curator named Bret Smallwood, a tall skinny fellow with a leather-and-silver bolo tie and a degree in art history from William and Mary. He was clearly unhappy with his job and was not hesitant to say so.

"I haven't got any budget to speak of," he said. "And how does one run a museum without a budget?"

"Must be tough," I said.

"I've had to abandon any hope of cataloguing this material," he said. "But most of it's trash anyway. Nobody around here has any sort of aesthetic sense."

"Where you from originally, Mr. Smallwood?"

"Wyoming originally," he said. "But everywhere really."

"I'm from around here," I said.

"Oh," he said. He began to stammer. "About what I said before... I...I didn't necessarily mean..."

"No offense taken," I said. "You mind if I plow around though the trash a bit?"

He handed me his flashlight. He'd turned on the overhead fluorescents but most of them weren't working. From the smell of things, mice had gnawed the wiring and gotten fried. "Feel free," he said.

I didn't find it. One look at all those piles and I was pretty sure I wouldn't, but I went at it hard for an hour or so and made myself sick breathing paper dust and mold. It would take weeks to sort through all those boxes and I'd had my fill of research.

After the library and the museum I felt pretty grungy and was hungry again and needed a shower. I thought about going home to my apartment, or to Lorrie's apartment, or else to my father's place, but the risk wasn't warranted. I didn't want to face my father, and Lorrie would want to talk. I found a skid-row room with reasonably clean sheets in downtown Bridgewater, at the Saint Christopher Hotel, and rented it for an entire week in advance for $240 bucks. I washed up as best I could and went out to dinner at Dunkin' Donuts. I had the open-faced hot turkey sandwich—which was pressed turkey from a can and white bread covered with pale brown gravy and zapped in a microwave. It didn't quite fill me up so I had a powdered jelly donut and coffee for dessert. It was the kind of meal that could kill you.

The waitress behind the counter was a little Asian girl about seventeen years old. She wore white tennis shoes and a ribbed polyester blouse. Her shoulder bones were as delicate as a dove's. I ignored the no-tipping sign and left her a couple of dollars. I had exactly one-hundred dollars left to live on for a week—assuming I got to live that long. She brightened like I'd made her day. I was glad that somebody was happy. Perhaps that was my true vocation. I could forget the detective business and simply wander around America, leaving tiny tips in places where they weren't expected.

Now I was at loose ends, but I sure had time to kill, so I went back to my room at the Saint Christopher to spend the evening studying the tax map. I spread it on the lumpy bed. It was a huge map, nearly five feet square, and once I'd read all the copyright markings and abbreviations and different-colored dotted lines, I concentrated on locating railroad tracks. What I discovered astounded me.

In the heart of downtown Bridgewater, running north and south with the tracks for a quarter of a mile or so, was a city owned right-of-way about two hundred feet wide. In the middle of it was a vacant lot where that burned-down railway station had already been completely bulldozed. There was nothing left but a switching yard linking a few industrial spur lines that paralleled the main tracks and extended past the city limits—north toward Boston and south toward NYC.

It didn't take a genius to figure out that such a right of way was worth money. Because whoever controlled it, controlled the pas sage of East Coast trains. If you wanted to ship by rail to or from Massachusetts, Vermont, New Hampshire, Maine, or on into the Canadian Maritime, you'd need a way to send freight cars through Bridgewater. Even a modest per-boxcar fee charged to everybody who wanted to use that short stretch of track would make the owners insanely rich.

And this was exactly the kind of thing that somebody—even a man in a position of political power like McLean—could have gotten himself killed over. And it was exactly the kind of thing that Bridgewater's current scumbag of a mayor would obviously have an abiding interest in.

Like every mayor the citizenry had elected since Jasper McLean, Hiram Silverstone was basically another crook on the take, but his media image was better crafted. His political campaigns were well funded and run by professionals, and, at least thus far, Silverstone hadn't personally been indicted for anything—not even after that old train station had gone up in flames, a crime to which the feds still couldn't directly tie him.

Some men could probably admire a guy whose values were that twisted. Although, actually, so far as my own unabashed admiration went, I felt an unaccustomed need for some restraint. For Silverstone and his city council cronies, values—except for monetary values—probably never even came into play. Even the "Law" with a capital L didn't matter much to them. It was Silverstone who told his police force to enforce whatever laws just so happened to support his own business interests. His "fiscally conservative" brand of public corruption was so essentially nihilistic that he could make even an old-school mobster like Sal Almonde look like a straight shooter. Almonde might be deadly, but he understood right from wrong. He was greedy and intelligent, but he wasn't amoral—although, so far as the real-world implications of my reasoning went, such hairsplitting distinctions were simply absurd. Kings or criminals, immoral or amoral, was there supposedly some difference?

CHAPTER *26*

By morning it was raining hard, another cold miserable day, when I could have been vacationing in Florida. Sleeping alone in a skid-row hotel wasn't helping my mood. I hadn't called Lorrie again and felt guilty about it. All night long I'd tossed and turned under my well-worn sheets until by daybreak I felt so jangled and queasy I didn't think I could hold down coffee. I pissed in the tiny enamel sink— the john was out in the hall—and sipped a little lukewarm tap-water to settle my stomach.

I decided it was time to report to Mrs. McLean—although I still wasn't entirely sure I should risk getting in touch with her. The longer I thought about it, the more I guessed that her phone-line was probably tapped. Sal Almonde wasn't one to leave details to chance, and I wasn't about to help him kill me by being careless. Maybe I'd do better by driving over there—but first I needed to call in another favor.

I used the pay phone in the hotel lobby to dial Dave Polanski at Dave's TV Repair. Dave and I went back a long way. I'd once walked—unarmed except for a case of warm Budweiser and a hundred dollars cash—into the downtown headquarters of the Bridgewater Hell's Angels chapter and walked back out again with Dave's naked and stoned-out-of-her-mind sixteen-year-old daughter slung over my shoulder like a sack of lumpy Idaho reds. Saving her sorry little white-trash ass had only cost me a few gray hairs, the case of beer, and the cash. The Angels had been agreeable because they figured she'd run right back to them as soon as she sobered up. But Dave had hustled her off to a detox center somewhere in New Haven and from there to an all-girls' college in West Virginia where the last thing I'd heard she was studying to be a pediatric nurse. Dave considered me her guardian angel.

For a few months afterwards I'd had a rush of detective business from blue-collar daddies who wanted me to find and save their runaway daughters from the clutches of one outlaw motorcycle club or another. I paid off bikers left and right and bought a whole lot of beer and carted out a dozen or so underage biker chicks, but most of their fathers had never followed through like Dave and their daughters had just run away again.

So after a while the referrals quit coming and the extra business fizzled out. Still, I'd made a name for myself with the Harley-Davison crowd as an up-front cash customer, and Dave still felt he owed me. I was happy to let him think so. Every once in a while I had to move something heavy, and he always let me borrow his van.

"Dave," I said. "Pete Lombardo. I'm calling because I need a favor."

"Anything thing you need, Petey."

"Can I borrow your van for a couple of hours this morning?"

"Sure, so long as you put some gas in it."

"You got it," I said, feeling guilty because I hadn't the last time. I hung up and drove over.

Dave's Electronic Shop was on the bad end of Franklin Avenue, in a small cinderblock building that occupied a corner lot. The front window was plate glass, but the glass was cracked and taped, and somewhere along the line Dave had added an accordion grate to discourage break-ins. The shop was terribly cluttered, with old TVs, stereos, VCRs, and computer monitors stacked up like cordwood. There was scarcely room to walk and not a free surface anywhere that wasn't littered with tiny screws and circuit boards and pieces of wire and loose transistors. Dave had old electronic hardware that went back almost to the time of Edison. Yet he stayed current enough to know how even the latest video games worked. I liked Dave as much as I liked anybody, but even by my lax standards he wasn't much of a businessman. He'd spend four hours finding a used part to fix an obsolete adding machine that any reasonable person would abandon as hopeless. Then he'd forget to charge the customer for his time. Dave was successful almost in spite of himself because he was honest and knew what he was doing and because people liked him. Not even in my unremembered dreams would I ever be as good a detective as he was a repairman. But then I usually had to deal with broken lives that wouldn't sit still long enough to be tinkered with. In a sense, even Lorrie had it easier, although her clients were generally more screwed up than mine.

Dave had the keys ready for me as soon as I walked in. I'd known the guy for what seemed like forever, yet every time I saw him I was always a little taken aback at first by how diminutive he was— less than five feet tall with child-sized hands and pale, pencil-thin arms. Winter or summer he wore baggy short-sleeved work shirts from one of those rental outfits with his name in yellow script above the pocket. The lenses in his black-framed eyeglasses were thick as the tops of canning jars.

"So how's the detective business going, Petey?" he asked.

"Fairly busy," I said.

He gestured at the cluttered shop. "Me too," he said. "I'm up to my ass in repairs, but you know, sometimes I wish I was out there fighting crime like you."

"Yeah," I said, "why's that?"

He looked suddenly sheepish, almost embarrassed. "You know, it's kind of exciting and all."

"I suppose," I said.

"Don't put yourself down."

"Well," I said. "I really appreciate the van. I'll remember to gas it up."

Dave looked embarrassed again." I was just joking about the gas."

"How's your daughter doing these days?"

He pulled out a photograph—she'd never been an especially good-looking girl. "She's a senior, now," he said. "Graduates in May." There was real pride in his voice and his eyes actually glistened. Hokey as hell, but oddly moving too.

"Glad to hear it," I said, and I was.

"Anything else I can do for you, kid?"

"As a matter of fact," I said, "you got anything to remedy a bugged phone?"

He smiled. We were talking his area of expertise now.

"I got just the thing you need," he said.

He rummaged around his cluttered shop until he came up with what looked to be a cheap plastic G.E. cassette player and a cracked electric Lady Remington razor duck-taped side by side to a good-sized piece of particle board with some extra transistors and a tiny transformer or two. The whole contraption was powered by a long extension cord with a two-pronged plug that Dave plugged into his workbench outlet.

"That's what I need?"

"Just drop this in and push play," he said. He had opened a workbench drawer and pulled out a cassette tape: *The Beach Boys Greatest Hits*.

I slid in the cassette and pushed the button. The player started to turn but I didn't hear anything.

"Bad volume control?"

"That's the beauty of it," Dave said. "Talking on the phone you won't ever know it's there—it's broadcasting on an inaudible frequency, but anybody who tries to listen with an electronic bug gets an earful," he hesitated. "Continuous loop. Debugs an entire room. Phone and all. Take it if you can use it."

I pulled the plug and grinned as I carried the gizmo outside in an oversized cardboard box and put it in Dave's van. I had a wonderful mental image of Bosco and Geno and Almonde huddled around a fancy receiver in that office above the funeral home. They were listening hard for cryptic meanings in the lyrics of "Little Surfer Girl."

Dave hadn't even asked when I'd be back. His van was an old six-cylinder Ford Econoline with *Dave's Electronic Repair* stenciled carefully on the side. I stopped at the corner Gas-n-Go and bought him a tank of regular, and for myself a cheap red baseball cap to go with my cheap sunglasses. From there I drove to Mrs. McLean's and went up her walk pushing a hand truck with Dave's contraption in the cardboard box and carrying an aluminum clipboard. I had my new baseball cap pulled low over my shades. She came to the door and opened it as far as the security chain would allow and still didn't recognize me—so I held up the clipboard. I'd written the words "Lombardo in disguise" on the sheet.

"Dave's TV repair," I said.

"Yes," she said. "Please come in."

I held a finger to my lips until I had plugged in my new debugger and flipped the toggle. Then I filled her in. I left out the scene with Geno and Bosco, but I told her about the bullets through my Escort and that I figured Almonde and the mob were behind her husband's death which had something to do with valuable railroad real estate. She listened carefully until I was done, then pulled out a hankie with lace embroidery around the edges.

"I always suspected it was something like that," she said between sniffles. Her eyes were red and continued to drip as we spoke. I couldn't help but admire her capacity for fidelity. For me, McLean was someone from history, a man who was only a public memory. For her, he might have died last week.

"I'm sorry," I said.

"It's appalling that they would threaten you," she said. "Perhaps it's time to call in the authorities."

"Knowing and proving are two different things," I said. "And your phone is probably bugged."

"Is that the purpose of that ugly contraption?"

"Sometimes ugly is beautiful," I said. "This thing ought to clean your line."

"And why do you suspect my phone is tapped?"

"Look," I said. "Right now all I have is motive. I don't have any evidence that your husband was really murdered or that greed had anything to do with it. And I'm not sure there's much hope of justice in the legal sense."

She nodded. "I see," she said. "Perhaps, then, you'd like to terminate the investigation?"

"I've been spending a lot of your money," I said. "In fact, it's nearly all gone."

She dropped her eyes again. "Lorrie was so right about you. You have a romantic temperament. Much like my late husband's. But one doesn't live for nearly nine decades and become a politician's widow and maintain many illusions about justice in the legal sense."

"So you want me to stay with the case?"

"Of course. And as for justice, I'll trust you'll do your best."

"Yeah," I said. "But I'm not about to try to take out Sal Almonde."

She almost seemed horror-stricken, but I could have also sworn that she had to work to suppress a smile. "Perish the thought."

"What exactly is it you want me to do then?"

"Perhaps we could exhume Jasper's body," she said. "I'm told forensic medicine has come a long way."

"All those years in the ground," I said. "I don't want to sound crude, but there's probably not much left of him."

"He's in the family mausoleum," she said. "And the casket was very expensive—supposedly air-tight."

I shrugged. "It might make a difference," I said.

"I've never believed it was carbon monoxide," she said. "He'd never deliberately sit still that long. It was a matter of character. Jasper was a doer."

I began to fidget.

"I'm obviously long-winded," she said. "I'll let you get back to work. I'll arrange the exhumation."

I stood up and took a few steps toward the door.

"Mr. Lombardo?"

"Yes?"

"Aren't you forgetting the television?"

I gave her a grin, then grabbed the hand-truck from the foyer where I'd parked it and unplugged the old-fashioned console in her living room and rolled the hand-truck underneath.

She held the door for me as I eased the console out. "Probably the picture tube," I said aloud, and wrestled it into the van and drove away.

I headed straight back to the St. Christopher, where I used the pay phone in the lobby to check back with Carlos Wayne.

"Carlos?"

"Peter, my boy. I was wondering when you'd be calling again."

"Bridgewater Land?"

"Not much, my boy. But some. A rather obscure real estate investment company. Fifty-one percent is owned by the city of Bridgewater, twenty-five percent held by a not-for-profit trust, the remaining twenty-four percent owned by a private for-profit corporation. The non-profit group is the University of Bridgewater. The for-profit corporation is a wholly owned subsidiary of another privately held company. No recent trades. No recent offers either. Bridgewater Land's assets consist entirely of a section of right-of-way currently leased to the New York-Connecticut railroad. That stretch is used constantly by Amtrack and various commercial freight lines. The railroad pays the pro-rated taxes, keeps the tracks in repair, and sends one dollar a year to Bridgewater Land."

"Doesn't sound like anything," I lied.

"The company was first incorporated in 1945 when it was probably necessary to uprade existing rail access to Bridgewater to support the war effort. Some private and public lands were combined into a single holding and rented out to the railroads in one of those rare examples of cooperation that were seemingly motivated by patriotic fervor. The first lease was for fifteen years—during which time the city of Bridgewater built the old train station and paid for it with public funds. The second lease was for fifty years—and is up for renewal again this year."

"And what do you suppose that renewed lease might be worth?"

"I really wouldn't presume."

"Hazard a guess."

"Well, billions of tons of rail freight do need to be moved some how. And thousands of commuters do need to get to work daily."

"You have a name on that wholly owned subsidiary?"

"You'll like this," Carlos said, "with your sense of the ironic."

"Hit me."

"Eternal Life Inc."

"I suppose that's ironic," I said.

"This is," said Carlos. "Almonde and Sons Mortuary Services owns Eternal Life Inc."

"Carlos," I said, "I could kiss you."

"Don't eroticize my dreams, boy. Ta-ta and be good." He hung up, beating me to a reply.

"I am good," I said, but I was already talking to a dead line.

CHAPTER *27*

I supposed I needed to see Mayor Hiram Silverstone next, which meant I was about to blow my cover entirely, such as it was, but I was nearly out of cash, and I really didn't want to ask Mrs. McLean for any more right now, and obviously I couldn't stay underground forever. And if there was anything I didn't need, it was another powerful enemy.

I'd already decided I'd try taking advantage of the Mayor's Open-Door-Tuesdays policy and attempt to convince him I was predisposed to be friendly. The November elections were now rapidly approaching and Silverstone was only slightly ahead in the polls, so he'd decided to make himself available to the good citizens of Bridgewater one afternoon a week—so that average city taxpayers would have an opportunity to speak directly to him, albeit briefly, about their mundane worries and pothole-sized concerns and without the need to make impossible-to-schedule appointments with the various reluctant-to respond city agencies.

Silverstone still had a private secretary to screen out the total crazies. And, of course, she'd made sure that representative flunkies from various city departments were also on hand to solve the most common constituent problems—so that in practice only about one in twenty citizens actually got in to see Mayor Silverstone in person. Nevertheless, this open door idea had proved incredibly popular with the electorate, and that shit still mattered in a democracy, I supposed.

Silverstone's well coifed secretary obviously didn't think much of my chances of actually seeing the Mayor—at least not when I first showed up at his office. She turned up her nose at me, sniffed, and examined her long, polished pink fingernails instead. Fortunately, I'd showered this morning, although I hadn't shaved in days, and there was already a long line of shabby and mostly elderly people waiting to patiently to see him. I was still wearing my Goodwill chinos and baseball cap, and I probably looked to her like a wino, but she did ask me very politely to write down my name and exactly what I wanted to see the mayor about on a 3x5 index card.

I took the card, borrowed a pen, and wrote down, after some initial hesitation, my real name, and then two words: Bridgewater Land before handing the card back to her. She examined what I'd written, frowned again, and asked me with a kind of snooty superiority, if this were about a zoning matter. This question took me back, but only for a minute.

"In a sense," I said. "But I'd make sure the Mayor sees this card immediately. If he's not suddenly interested in meeting me, I'll leave without a fuss".

She frowned and asked me to have a chair, but carried the card to the inner sanctum.

I took a seat in a double row of metal folding chairs that had set up for waiting taxpayers, who, truth be told, were a rather pathetic looking bunch. They were basically all very poor people who were being patronized by flunkies. In fact, if I didn't know better, I'd have sworn that a least some of my fellow supplicants had been sent over by central casting to audition as extras for a remake of *The Grapes of Wrath*. More than half of them were old and either grossly overweight or else bony-ass skinny. Some needed to use canes or aluminum walkers to get to or from the folding chairs and any number of these also wore hearing aids and spoke too loud so that it was easy for me to listen to their whispered conversations around the waiting room, conversations that seemed to be mainly about how they couldn't afford to stay in their own homes after the city's recent tax reassessment (which I also vaguely remembered my father bitching about last month) and so had recently been forced to choose between paying their property taxes and either the various prescription drugs they needed to stay alive or else between sufficient food or fuel enough to warm their decrepit bodies.

For a minute or so, it was almost too damn sad. Sad enough to make me feel like these people were my true people, salt of a poisoned earth, helpless kindred who somebody needed to protect from the Hiram "High Hopes" Silverstones of the world, and I was one of them forever.

But this was sentimental dribble, and down deep I knew it. I had so little in common with these simple-minded oldsters that we'd probably hate each other's guts if we got to talking honestly.

The trouble was that it was hard to ignore them. There wasn't even a rack of old fishing magazines to choose from while we waited, and I sat here brooding about how very little any one of us really mattered in the grand cosmic scheme of things.

Fortunately, this bipolar tango between compassion and self pity only went on for something under five minutes before the secretary came out again and waved me to the head of the line. I looked at my fellow citizens and smiled sheepishly, but I barely had time to collect my thoughts before I was ushered inside.

The Honorable Hiram Silverstone gave me a wide grin. "Mr. Lombardo, what can I do for you?"

"Run the railroad," I said.

"How's that?"

"I've started a one-man grass-roots effort to return the City to long-term financial solvency and get you re-elected by a landslide this November."

"Sounds good," he said. "Glad to have your support."

"I could care less what kind of deals you cut, Hiram," I said. "But you need to tell your buddy Sal Almonde not to poison the grass where those roots are trying to grow."

Suddenly Mayor Silverstone wasn't smiling any longer. He didn't know who I was or who I represented, and he probably didn't care, but bravado and namedropping had immediately convinced him that I must be some kind of player, and that I obviously knew something about something.

I watched him stiffen. He was choosing his words very carefully as if he were afraid I might be wired.

"My administration has long had a policy of supporting the job- and tax-revenue producing engine of small business."

"Bridgewater Land," I said, "is a public private partnership."

"Well, I'm glad to know that you support our initiative."

"I'm not asking either you or Sal you to fertilize the grass. I'm asking you to let it grow untended."

"And your interest in all this?"

"None of yours," I said. "But I was an English major back in college, and I've got half a dozen letters written and researched and ready to send to the various media outlets—you don't own all of them."

"I see," he said.

"Talk to Sal," I said, and reached out to pat his pin-striped shoulder. "See what you can do."

CHAPTER 28

I wanted my big guns. I wanted them the way a kid wants a Nutty Buddy ice cream bar or a Marine just finishing boot camp wants an easy woman. All that talk with Mrs. Mclean about exhuming dead bodies made me feel corporeal and expendable. And after talking tough to Silverstone, I needed to feel armed.

It was raining again. By the time I dropped off Dave's van and unloaded the TV in his shop and picked up my rental car, I was seriously hungry. I regretted skipping breakfast and wanted someplace anonymous to pig out. I settled for the Mermaid Tavern by the airport—in part because I liked the Shakespearean name but also because they made a great Reuben sandwich and sold cold draft beer for two bucks a frosted mug.

The tavern was dark inside—but it was a very deliberate kind of darkness. The Mermaid was where the salaried office supervisors at the Helicopter plant went on their long lunch hours to start affairs with their secretaries. I had two cold beers and a huge sandwich and a side order of fries with the vitamin-rich skins left on them. The good meal cost less than fifteen dollars including the tip. I felt fortified. I bought myself a cheap cigar for the drive to the airport.

It was still raining out when I pulled into long-term parking. I found my Escort and had just unlocked the driver's door and reached inside to pull my .38 from beneath the seat when I had a terrible piece of luck: Bosco drove by in the Buick, probably to make sure my vehicle was still there. Two minutes either way and I'd have missed him, but all my precautions were for nothing because he saw me, hit the brakes, and backed up. I came up with both guns. The shotgun in one hand and the pistol in the other and the cigar between my lips like Big Al Capone. I pointed them like I meant business when Bosco began to get out of the car. He thought better of it quickly and just sat there idling and making calls on a Blackberry before he drove away.

His leaving didn't comfort me. I'd have preferred some sort of confrontation with witty dialogue and complicated insults. The worst thing that could happen would be to have everything become businesslike. If Sal Almonde chose to ignore Silverstone's sensitivities and put out a professional contract, I'd be hit by someone with killing skills so far out of my league that he'd make Geno and Bosco look like a Cub Scouts. If I was going to keep any kind of edge, I had to keep on keeping on. Although it would take some serious bluffing, I had to get Almonde to take me seriously, as a threat he'd have to live with. If I had to get nasty about it, I would. Romantic types didn't last in Bridgewater. You had to be able to swim for miles in the sewage. I waited for few minutes until no one in the parking lot was close enough to watch as I transferred all my guns from one car to another, and locked up. I hiked to the terminal, found a phone, and called Almonde. I got Geno.

"Put the old man on," I said. "Tell him it's personal."

Geno recognized my voice and cursed. I heard him repeat my message to someone. I waited, and after a minute or two Almonde was on the line.

"So," he said. "Back from vacation so soon?"

"I'd like to arrange another pow-wow," I said. "Perhaps sometime later this afternoon?"

"About what?"

"Phones are funny," I said. "They make me nervous."

"A lot of things make you nervous. What? You don't like warm weather?"

"Makes you sweat."

"You ought to come down to Oysterman's Health Club this

afternoon. I'll show you what it means to sweat."

"Sure," I said. "Maybe I'll take the train?"

"Train?"

"I figured I'd ride before ticket prices went up. But maybe it doesn't go there."

"Maybe it doesn't go a lot of places? Maybe you shouldn't care where it goes?"

"Maybe it doesn't concern me," I said. "Maybe I'll think long and hard about that."

"Yeah, maybe you'd better think."

"Around three at the health club?"

"Sure," Almonde said. "Come on down."

"One more thing, Mr. Almonde."

"What's that?"

"Mrs. McLean," I said. "She's having the body exhumed. It wasn't carbon monoxide."

There was silence for a minute.

"The dead sleep better when they're not disturbed."

"Yeah, the dead can disturb you," I said. "Sometimes it's better not to make a guy dead."

"I've heard that argument made," he said softly. "I've never thought much of it."

"Three o'clock," he said, and hung up.

I put my head against the pay phone. I'd bought time but it had cost me. Sal Almonde wasn't as easily frightened as Mayor Silverstone, who, after all, was running for re-election, but I hoped I'd made Almonde curious—just curious enough to wait.

CHAPTER 29

Sal Almonde looked good on the treadmill. Designer sneakers. L.L. Bean sweatshirt. Cotton headband. Thick white terrycloth towel. A thin sheen of perspiration glistening on his ruddy face. Perhaps afterwards there'd be a rubdown, a shower, and a glass of fresh-squeezed carrot juice.

My sneakers were old-fashioned Converse hi-tops, bright red ghetto stompers that were actually fashionable again but had probably been left to dry rot in a warehouse for twenty years or more before they'd turned up in a bin at that downtown Salvation Army store where I was suddenly becoming regular customer. I had on some cutoff jeans that somebody sloppy had painted in and an extra-large polyester t-shirt with a picture of Bullwinkle the Moose with a mortarboard between his antlers and the words Whatsamatter U. In cracked plastic lettering across the front. I looked ragged and felt worse. And like a traitor Bridgewater U, my true alma mater. I had only been allowed inside by the spa's manager, a condescending aerobics freak in green Robin Hood tights, because I'd told him I was Almonde's guest. The manager seemed terribly put out. I had a tea towel in my belt loop so I yanked it out and snapped it at his tights a few times to be obnoxious as I followed him through the weight room.

"Sorry to disturb you, Mr. Almonde, but this gentleman insists he's here as your guest."

Almonde looked up at me and didn't seem surprised. "Yeah," he said. "Maybe." Then he waited, not saying a word until the manager turned and left us.

"Looking great, Sal," I said.

"*Sal* again?" he said. "Are we really that familiar?"

"Each man is a piece of the continent," I said. "A part of the main—or maybe I just read that shit somewhere."

"What main would that be?" Almonde asked. He continued to walk the treadmill.

I took up a position at a Nautilus machine right beside him, having to adjust the weights first so I could move them without much effort.

"Maybe it's more like we're all riding a train. Together in one big compartment."

"You keep mentioning trains. You hung up on trains?"

"Must be my subconscious. Too much thinking along certain lines."

"Say what you come to say," Almonde said. "I don't find you amusing."

I clanged the weights up and down a few times. "Trains make a lot of noise. It's hard to think clearly."

"You better come see me when you got something to communicate," Almonde said. He elevated the treadmill until it became a hill he was climbing.

"If the city was in dire enough financial straits, Silverstone might want to squeeze the railroads extra hard when their lease is up."

Almonde smiled and increased the speed on his treadmill so that he had to jog to keep up. I couldn't help but admire his stamina. "Maybe you got some point to make?"

"I think you had Jasper McLean killed fifty years ago," I said. "Or maybe it was your father still in charge back then."

"Yeah?" he said. He seemed disinterested. "Why would he do that?" He wasn't even breathing hard.

"Probably because Mclean refused to stick it to the railroads directly—probably because he knew they'd turn around and screw the daily commuters and small manufacturers to recover the difference. Basically, the city had the railroads over a barrel. McLean gave up the short-term advantage and got them to agree to link freight rates and ticket prices to some sort of flexible formula that limited profits, all in exchange for a favorable long-term lease. Hardball in the public interest, and for decades it worked pretty well. Only now that lease is about up."

"You got a wonderful imagination. But you ever hear of slander?"

"Just between us," I said. "Lawyers annoy me. Even smart ones like Silverstone."

Almonde nodded and began to jog even faster, pushing the machine to its limits.

"Actually, I think you've done everything in your power to fuck up this city," I said, "just so they'd play along with you when it was lease renewal time. I bet, for instance, the city's exclusive owner ship of that old train station complicated things. Maybe just enough to have somebody burn it down. Meanwhile, if security stays lax at Bridgewater Airport, sooner or later something incredibly shitty happens out there too, and afterwards the insurance costs make moving air-freight through Bridgewater so prohibitively expensive that no airline can hope to compete with the trains—no matter what kind of tonnage fee the Mayor decides to charge."

He flicked a switch and stopped the treadmill abruptly. "Like I said, you got an active imagination. You'll start blaming me for the traffic jams on I-95 next."

"I didn't imagine being shot at."

He turned to face me and dabbed at his face with his towel. "Say you got an annoying insect. A mosquito. A horse fly. First you take a swing at it, and maybe you miss. So then you get to thinking— maybe I'm too harsh, maybe the fly's got a right to live. So you open up a window, you try to shoo it out. But the fly won't go. So you get yourself a swatter and splat it."

"What if the fly's too quick for you?"

"Then you find the shit pile where it eats and poison its food."

"The metaphor's getting strained, Sal," I said. "Are you trying to tell me that the boys got a little impulsive when they air-conditioned my Escort and that you're sorry?"

He shook his head and laughed. "Personally, I don't believe in regret," he said. "But boys will be boys."

"Especially Geno," I said. "He's always going to be a boy."

"Some guys never grow up," he agreed. "You think that old lady's gonna pay you if she's dead?"

"Hadn't thought about that," I said. And I hadn't.

"Or maybe you think she can somehow pay you if you're dead?"

"Highly unlikely."

"So why talk to me? Because so far as I'm concerned, you're dead. I only met with you again because I thought you were maybe clever."

"I put out a fused contract on your grandkids," I said. "I had enough ready cash left to pay for five little dead bambinos, and I paid in advance, but I didn't specify which five. My death lights the fuse. You can't protect all of them—because they're a part of the main too. So how's that for clever?"

He was livid. "What?"

I'd only said it to say something, but now I had to elaborate. "Maybe you think it's the good old days, with families and kids off limits. Maybe you think you're immune to pain because you're old-time Cosa Nostra with political pull and hired muscle and a huge law firm on retainer to make sure your shit smells sweet. But you got lots and lots of grandkids and dead people got nothing to lose."

"You stupid little prick," Almonde said. "You think you can threaten me?"

"I'm basically as harmless as a fly," I said.

He shook his head. He actually looked bemused.

"I'm a fuck-up, Sal," I continued. "A wild card. If I don't stay alive, I can't cancel the contract. And a handful of little bambinos don't get to ride the choo-choo."

His face was wonderful. "What exactly is it you want?"

I took a deep breath. For the first time I felt a certain shift in our relationship.

"Let's do lunch next week," I said. "There's plenty for everybody if nobody gets greedy."

"I used to know guys like you," Almonde said softly. He smiled.

"Hell, once upon a time I used to *be* a guy like you. I guess I'm getting mellow and respectable in my dotage."

I extended my hand and to my amazement he shook it.When Sal Almonde smiled it scared the crap out of me.

CHAPTER

I went back to my apartment and collected three days of news-paper deliveries from my all-weather plastic box, climbed the narrow inside stairs, unlocked the door, went to bed, and took a nap—a calculated risk. Almonde wouldn't try to off me until he'd determined if there really *was* a contract on his grandkids and, if so, with whom. I'd made a single phone call from a pay phone outside his health club—I called a local Hell's Angels chapter, where they knew me from the old days, and ordered up a parade. I gave them Almonde's daughter's address in Westport and offered a hundred bucks a man if they'd ride around her block twenty-five times or so. Absolutely legal, but I figured they'd drive Almonde's people wild.

His organization was so well insulated he no longer had direct contacts with such groups. It would take him a while to figure out the bottom line. In the meantime I could catch a few Zs. I slept for maybe an hour before a ringing phone jarred me awake, and I fumbled with the receiver.

"Did you threaten Sal Almonde's grandkids?" It was Lorrie.

"Only in passing."

"What kind of man are you?" She sounded shrill.

"Sleepy."

"Sometimes I think I don't know you at all."

"Does anybody really know another person?"

"Peter! You wouldn't really have someone kill his grandkids, would you?"

"What is reality?" I said. "I'm a little confused."

"I don't want to get into specifics here, but Sal and I were working on trust. Social integration. A sense of the human community. Your threatening his grandkids probably set his emotional development back twenty years."

"So sorry," I said. "Sorry to be a counterproductive influence on Almonde's therapy."

"You're not the least bit sorry."

"Frankly, I know exactly who the bell tolls for, and I wouldn't mind if that greasy old motherfucker were to die of a heart attack and leave all his dirty money to the Pope."

"I see," Lorrie said. "You're insane."

"Look," I said. "Can I come over and explain? Maybe we'll eat vegetarian tacos and rent a foreign movie."

"I think not," Lorrie said.

"You're pissed?"

"Some detective," she said, and hung up.

I felt like killing someone. I felt like firing a gun. I wanted guts and blood and gore on my walls. It wasn't a directed anger, and certainly not focused on Almonde's grandkids, but the strong emotion was something to savor. I'd really gone and handled things. I'd managed to make personal with Almonde what had previously been only business. As soon as he found out there wasn't a contract on his grandkids, he'd have me killed just to streamline things. No trips to Florida. No warning shots through cars. And to top it all off, I'd put Mrs. McLean's life in danger.

All I knew for certain was that I couldn't lie in bed and hope for things to get much better. I flung off the covers, got up, made some strong coffee, scrambled myself three large eggs, and dropped two slices of whole wheat bread in the toaster.

Four days worth of unread newspapers were still waiting for me to read, so I unrolled yesterday's issue on my kitchen table and scanned the classifieds, the comics, Dear Abby, and my daily horoscope: "Your future will be eventful." Finally, I turned to the financial pages to see how the stocks I didn't own were doing and saw Almonde's smiling face topping a two-column headline: "Local Businessman Acquires Gas Storage Facility." At first, I could barely focus. I was still stupid with rage, but as I ate my eggs I managed to read the article closely. It was a feature piece, a human interest story that teased like soft-core porn rather than providing clarity.

BRIDGEWATER—Sal Almonde, chief executive officer of Almonde Enterprises, Inc., announced the recent acquisition of a natural gas storage facility previously owned by Connecticut Petroleum Products. The facility, located in an area of the city zoned for industrial use, has been a focus of controversy in recent years. Some residents in adjoining neighborhoods have complained about the environmental impact of gas storage on air quality, and others expressed concerns about security procedures which they believe do little to protect them from the ever-present chance of fire and explosion. Last year a newly-formed neighborhood watchdog group forced CPP to submit to yearly inspections by state health personnel who examined the aging tank for rust and possible leaks, and required that the company surround the tank's perimeter with a barbed-wire fence to protect the aging structure from potential problems. "If that tank ever blows, it'll take half the East Side with it," said Lamar Long, head of the neighborhood group that has opposed continued use of the facility. A CPP spokesperson explained the sale of the tank by saying, "We were looking for a buyer to take over the facility so that we could concentrate on more profitable areas of our distribution system." But where one company saw risk another saw opportunity. "We're positioning ourselves for further local acquisitions," said Anthony Bosco, AE's official spokesperson. "We believe in Bridgewater and investing in Bridgewater. This town's been good to us, and we'd never do anything to endanger the people who live and work here."

I read the article closely, and then I read it again. It didn't make much sense. Why would Almonde saddle himself with an old storage tank that was basically an industrial accident waiting to happen? Even supposing he could coax a few more years of storage out of it, sooner or later that tank would reach the end of its usefulness. It would probably have to be emptied and dismantled and handled as hazardous waste, and that alone could cost big bucks. It wasn't a good investment in any way I understood the word, but Almonde had acquired it—not for altruistic reasons either, no matter what the article said.

I wasn't doing much else anyway, so I decided to drive out there and eyeball the thing. I hadn't seen the tank up close for years—not since I was a kid and it had figured prominently in my consciousness in a way it didn't anymore.

Back when we'd lived in that duplex on George Street, I could see the tank from my bedroom window—it was half a block away. I couldn't have been more than six or seven—because it was before my mother left us—when I'd realized that any punk firebug with a two-cent book of matches could spark a massive fireball that would incinerate our entire neighborhood along with everyone I'd ever loved.

I'd mentioned the tank to my father once; he'd heard me out at length, and he didn't try to convince me otherwise. He'd simply sighed and patted me on the head. But it wasn't long afterwards that he bought the split-level and we'd moved.

Back then, Bridgewater's elementary schools were still holding atom-bomb-warning drills twice a year—to prepare the kids to deal with a Hiroshima-sized mushroom cloud by crouching beneath their desks.

Those ridiculous drills had already gone on for nearly a decade, and ultimately it had taken the efforts of some politically-savvy PTA parents to convince a change-adverse school board that—since everybody within five-hundred miles of Bridgewater would be instantly fried in any nuclear strike by an I.C.B.M. equipped with multiple H-bomb warheads, and since New York City was very likely to be targeted and was only fifty miles away—such warning drills were unnecessarily upsetting to both the kids and their teachers.

And so, finally, the schools simply stopped holding warning

drills—and frankly I'd kind of missed them. With that huge storage tank always in the background of my awareness, I'd already become so accustomed to the idea of dying at any moment—of being reduced to bone and ash by something I couldn't control—that living with the bomb had seemed like business as usual, and those drills had been a welcome break from class-work.

Actually, at this moment I felt entirely ready for something apocalyptic to happen. I liked the feeling. I was improvising, following a whim. I was old enough to know I wasn't especially sensitive or noble and no longer felt obligated to pretend. Detectives in novels were nearly always much better human beings than the people they were up against, but I wasn't sure I could make that claim. Right about now I'd kill Almonde without compunction to save my skin, and he would surely do the same. If a punk burglar were to break into my attic apartment tonight I'd probably waste his ass to save my sixty-nine-dollar stereo system, and from Almonde's perspective I was a punk who had tampered in his private affairs. If it came down to dying at the hands of Almonde or the religious creeps and I was anywhere near the tank, I'd send in a round of buckshot and take half of Bridgewater with me.

CHAPTER 31

Up close the tank looked as beat up and time-ravaged as the tired body of a sixty-year old hooker. Reaching such a decrepit state had probably taken years of continuous bribery of public safety inspectors. From a distance the tank was just a big metal cylinder painted sky blue with a white band at the top. But up close I could see how the metal had corroded and pitted, how scales of rust had been repainted so many times that it was probably old paint as much as anything that was holding the shell together. There was also a rotten smell to it, the acrid reek of petroleum-fouled gravel and poisoned soil.

The tank was so huge that everything around it was in permanent shadow—the pumps and turn-wheels, the enormous relief valves, the tall chain-link fence that surrounded the entire complex, and the railroad spur line and siding where tank cars could load and unload. But the minute I saw those tracks, I immediately understood why Almonde had bought the place. It was potentially another way to move rail cars through town.

Almonde obviously didn't give a rat's ass about the storage facility. He could empty the tank, cut it up for scrap iron. It was the spur line that was valuable. If he could, somehow, link it together with a handful of other decrepit downtown properties, which in all likelihood he'd already acquired, he'd have leverage.

Almonde had to assume that, since the City of Bridgewater was the majority stock owner of Bridgewater Land, Mayor Silverstone would get to negotiate privately with the freight lines, and that whatever public deal might ultimately be cut, there'd be a private perk for Hiram, and potentially a big cash bribe, one that Eternal Life Inc.—nor Islamic Brightness for that matter—would never see a piece of.

And so for this moment, this one brief shining moment, Sal Almonde, the Islamic cultists, and the much abused taxpayers of Bridgewater shared a common threat and a common purpose. It was in everybody's best interest to keep Mayor Silverstone's private negotiations with the railroads above board and his opportunities for private graft within reason. It would actually be best if Silverstone were re-elected because that way he wouldn't need to try to get a big hunk of dirty money up front.

There was, as I'd recently informed Sal Almonde, plenty for everybody, but acquiring that ancient spur line was Almonde's way of hedging his bets. Almonde and Islamic Brightness together controlled only a minority interest in Bridewater Land, but if Almonde didn't entirely like the public deal that the Silverstone wanted to cut, he could offer the railroads another way to move their freight hrough town, an alternative deal that left Bridgewater Land out of the loop. Almonde obviously couldn't go too far with exercising this option or he'd piss off Silverstone's political supporters and the Islamic Brightness people too, but as an up-for reelection incumbent, Silverstone's had his political record to consider. As a "fiscal conservative" he couldn't very well oppose the rights of property owners to do whatever they wanted with privately owned land.

One way or another, Almonde was about to make a killing.

I took a deep breath of foul air and held it in my lungs like a hit off a joint, just to see what it would do. I had to give Almonde credit. He was the one man in a million who could see a place like this as an opportunity, who had the energy and imagination to seize life by the short hairs and execute an intricate plan, to wring money from the corrupt political heart of a post-industrial wasteland. It was essentially a creative act—and like all acts of creativity, more or less redemptive. I had enough of the failed artist in me to admire artistic types to a degree that they didn't deserve. If imagination was redemptive, what exactly was redeemed? Why was I thinking about a character like Almonde in spiritual terms?

I could certainly understand why Lorrie wanted to be his therapist. He was both father-confessor and an imaginative man with solid values but without taboos or much of a conscience—somebody who could say or do or forgive anything. At bottom, Hiram Silverstone was simply a smart political crook who would sell whatever he had to sell.

Sal Almonde was something more. The old bastard was special. He got under your skin, Almonde did, and my plans for mass destruction suddenly seemed pretty paltry. I might talk a good game when I was talking to myself, but I was really no more capable of killing Almonde's grandkids than I was of blowing up the storage tank and incinerating my old neighborhood. Almonde, on the other hand, was entirely capable of murder without regret, and some sick part of me thoroughly admired him for that.

I needed to get going. If I wanted to stay alive, I needed to hold something in my poker hand a bit more playable than empty threats and a holocaust I wouldn't start. I needed to solve the details of McLean's murder fast, and hanging around in the shadow of a leaky gas tank wouldn't help me. The trouble was that I couldn't keep all the details straight inside my head. I wasn't sure why.

Maybe it was almost too simple. A Mafia don, a nearly bankrupt city, a corrupt mayor, a university controlled by Islamic cultists. Even Carlos would acknowledge that these were mighty strange bed fellows. But the motive was profit, and anybody could understand profit. The Bridgewater Land Corporation would soon be sitting pretty—because this time when that lease came up for renewal there wouldn't be a Socialist mayor to care who got exploited. The lease would be renewed, and the big railroads would pay dearly. They would stall for a while and evoke the public interest, but in the end they would pay—and then pass their costs on.

Ultimately, the added costs of moving rail traffic through down town Bridgewater would come to be thought as a kind of nuisance fee, a petty tax, the price of doing business.

But now what? And so what? These were the paired questions that haunted me like a nightmare about a sexual encounter with Siamese twins. Yet these were the questions I kept asking myself as I drove around Bridgewater, hoping for some brilliant insight—like a Buddhist monk soaked in gasoline and getting ready to strike a match. The big old Pontiac was the perfect car for such meditations. I'd even gotten used to the moldy smell of the upholstery. When the streets were dry, the car practically drove itself. I fiddled with the push-button radio and found nothing but talk shows and top-forty. A passing car blinked headlights at me, and I turned mine on. Evening in Bridgewater—I'd been orbiting so far out that I'd lost track. I turned onto side streets where piles of demolition rubble, old appliances, sofas with torn armrests, and soggy mattresses blocked nearly every sidewalk. To save money and avoid fiscal ruin, the city had suspended bulk-item trash disposal over a year ago. In the least affluent neighborhoods, even the garbage trucks for household waste no longer made regular rounds. In the more community-minded areas on the north side of town, homeowners paid the young, marginally-employed owners of pickup trucks to haul away their castoff appliances and broken furniture and dump such shit in the empty lots downtown, or else they braved the county landfill in their Broncos and mini-vans. But the ghetto crowd just left the big trashy items on the curb where they collected in huge piles that became homes for rats and training grounds for child arsonists.

I turned down another street where a big four-story granite-and-cement building that had once been a locally-owned savings-and-loan had been left half demolished by a wrecking ball and crane. For a while, in the 1990s there had been talk of revitalizing down town Bridgewater's business district by building legal gambling casinos—Sal Almonde had been involved in that brainstorming session too, I'd bet. But the city already had a Jai Alai fronton operated by the mob, and the state government had a stake in a huge upstate casino run by some affirmative-action Indians, who had somehow convinced the governor's office that they were already losing money and didn't need any additional competition. Anyway, the savings and loan building was being demolished and pretty soon there'd be another vacant lot where Bridgewater's residents could toss their trash.

Motive. Motive. Motive. I kept thinking about motive. I had plenty of motive. I'd had that almost from the beginning, but I still didn't have linkage, evidence, or anything resembling proof of wrong doing. I kept driving around in circles. The longer I stayed outside in the cold, the more I began to feel frantic and paranoid. Sooner or later, Almonde would realize that his grandkids weren't in real danger and have me turned into dogmeat. I could go to the Bridgewater police, but they wouldn't do anything. I could imagine how the cops would laugh if I tried to show them my Escort with wine-cork plugs in the roof. The local constabulary might prevent a armed burglary if they saw one in progress, but they certainly weren't going to hassle a solid citizen like Almonde who lunched with the chief of police and the mayor once a week. Besides, the city had everything to gain from screwing the big railroads because the city owned the lion's share of Bridgewater Land. A win-win situation. And I was caught between the winners.

Obviously, I needed to make my peace with someone—with Almonde, presumably, or failing that, with my client, Mrs. McLean, or with my father, or with Lorrie, or with myself. Chances were better than fifty-fifty that I'd be dead very shortly, and I didn't want to leave loose ends.

CHAPTER 32

Mrs. McLean was easiest so I figured I'd start with her. After that I'd go see my father and then Lorrie. As someone likely to be dead, and consequently squeamish about asking anyone for money, I'd nevertheless resolved to ask Mrs. McLean for another five hundred dollars. I figured I'd lay the cash on my father so he could use it for my funeral. Besides, my bank account was now completely and utterly empty again—and I'd need to live until I died. Which was, truth be told, why I had so much trouble cashing checks. It was too late in the day to bother with disguises, so I drove right over to Mrs. McLean's mansion and pounded on her door until she let me in.

"Mr. Lombardo," she said.

"Mrs. McLean," I said. "I basically stopped by to tell you I may be terminating the investigation shortly."

Her astonishment was strictly formal. "But, Mr. Lombardo," she said, "it's been progressing so nicely. They've finished the exhumation and Japser's casket was indeed airtight."

"Progressing nicely," I said, "except I may be dead myself shortly."

"I fully expect the pathologist's report on Jasper's tissue samples any day."

"How'd you arrange all that so fast?" I asked.

"I have old friends in the state government who brought the matter to the attention of the SBI crime lab."

"Jesus," I said. "With those kinds of connections you don't need me. Hell, you never needed me!"

"Perhaps there'll be some residual poison in his system," she said quickly. "Besides the carbon monoxide, I mean."

I nodded but I found that last detail a bit too precise for my taste. The old lady doth speculate too much.

I smiled vaguely. I made myself hold the smile. "Mrs. McLean," I said, "I suspect you know a good deal more than you've told me."

"Suspicions are wonderfully intriguing, Mr. Lombardo, but I'm paying you to discover facts. Be off with you. I'll not hear any more about your giving up the investigation."

"Mrs. McLean," I said, "Sal Almonde may have me killed. And you're talking absolute shit in a phony Irish accent."

"Nonsense." Her face became stern, "Sal Almonde isn't as cold-hearted as he pretends to be. I've known him a long time."

"I see," I said. She seemed a little agitated and I didn't want her having a stroke.

"Very well, then," she said and stood up slowly. "I'm about to steep some black raspberry tea. But we will certainly terminate this line of inquiry. Will you stay?"

"Perhaps another time," I said and went out.

I got back to my rented car and banged the steering wheel with my fist a few times, hard enough to hurt my hand. I hadn't even asked her for the money. I started the engine. I'd certainly made a mess of that encounter, but I'd come away with some suspicions that started me thinking again.

My father was next. He was sitting in his huge chair, watching reruns of a TV series in which a lady mystery novelist from a small town in coastal Maine solved a murder a week without breaking as sweat. The network advertised the series as a lighthearted murder mystery.

Dad didn't even bother to turn off the set when I told him it was likely I'd be dead by tomorrow. We sat there and watched TV together for a while.

He shook his head. "Dead by tomorrow, huh?" A commercial touting feminine-hygiene was on the screen now—a douche that supposedly kept women's crotches fresh as a mountain stream. I wondered vaguely if writing copy for such products might have been my ultimate fate if I hadn't been kicked out of college all those years ago for directing that porno-film. I also thought again about Andy Burnside, my Dad's old advertising buddy, and how, like him, what a terribly paltry legacy I'd leave to show for the time I'd lived on planet earth. *Thanks, I needed that.*

"It could happen," I said. "There are all kinds of rotten ways to die"

"It's a doggy-dog world," my father agreed. "But that's all it's ever been."

"I think you mean dog-*eat*-dog, Pop."

"Whatever," he said.

It was only when I pulled out my empty wallet and began to talk specifically about the high cost of funerals that he got interested enough to listen closely. I told him that whatever he decided, he was not under any circumstances to hire Sal Almonde's mortuary to deal with my dead carcass—no matter what kind of deal they offered. He hit the mute button on the remote, and against my better judgment, I laid out the whole case for him.

He listened carefully for a while, and when I was done he leaned back in his lounge chair so that his feet came up. He burped and grinned like he'd solved the riddle of the sphinx.

"The old lady's hiding something," he said.

"No shit," I said.

"So all you got to do is find out what and why."

I tried to keep my voice calm. "And how do I do that, Pop?"

"That's your trade, not mine. When I was your age, I had a steady job with Uncle Sam."

"So long, Pop," I said.

"Take-a-tissy," he said. He grabbed the remote and turned on the sound again. "Be careful out there."

Good advice. I refolded my empty wallet, pocketed it, and headed back out to my car. I had nothing to leave my father. In fact, I was pissed off enough to stick him with the burial bill. Or maybe he'd have me cremated. It wouldn't cost that much. Or for all I cared he could toss me in a vacant lot downtown. Or maybe the hit man

Almonde hired would be such a consummate professional that my remains would never be found. Ashes to ashes, dust to dust. Morbid thoughts. Or maybe I'd simply live forever and spite them all, the bastards!

Lorrie's apartment ought to have been my next stop. But she was probably still ticked off at me. So instead I stopped at the Nomad bar, where they knew me as a regular, and where Bill Morton, the late-evening bartender, would let me run a bar tab and pay at the end of the month, and where, if I were dead, the management would likely (if begrudging) have to eat said tab, so I ordered a scotch and soda.

If I somehow managed to live long enough to pay my monthly bar bill, life itself would be a cause for celebration. So I had two drinks. Actually, I had eleven or twelve drinks, and, finally, around midnight, Bill wisely cut me off and asked me if I needed a cab. I told him I didn't, but I stopped off yet again, this time to sober up, over soft-scrambled eggs at the State Street Diner, where I had apple pie, vanilla ice cream, and coffee with half-and-half for dessert.

I lingered a while over the coffee. A man who feels condemned to death doesn't worry about clogged arteries. The waitress was a tall, often-divorced woman named Tessie, who supported three kids and had very bad taste in husbands. She was someone I also knew well because I often ate there on her shift after a long night of barhopping. The evening rush was over, and she didn't charge me for the pie because she said it was stale. She zapped it in the microwave. It tasted fine to me, so I left her an extra dollar. A man who feels condemned doesn't pinch pennies either.

After eating, I felt better, so I took a chance and visited, albeit briefly, my own apartment, where I grabbed a bottle of dry, white Australian wine from my avocado-colored fridge. Next, I wandered into the 24-hour Pathmark on upper Main Street—where they sold cheap flowers from a glass case in the produce section. I found a bouquet called a wildflower potpourri for $7.95 and ran it by the cashier. For all her feminist sophistication, Lorrie melted when I brought her flowers and wine—or maybe she just liked me playing the ridiculous role of suitor.

Either way, I fully expected she'd forgive me for causing Sal Almonde to backslide when I explained that my threat was an empty one and that Sal Almonde's grandkids weren't really in any danger. I was even secretly entertaining warm and fuzzy notions that Lorrie and I would end up in the sack tonight and that tomorrow morning she'd use her influence as Almonde's therapist to help me arrange another meeting where we'd somehow both convince him that I deserved to be left alive. Then, with any luck at all, the SBI might even find something at the crime lab that would be so potentially incriminating that he'd be forced to let me live my stupid life for reasons other than misplaced loyalty to Lorrie

These thoughts were still mulling around in my head at two a.m. when I finally pulled onto Lorrie's block and saw the revolving lights of an ambulance and two squad cars flashing in the dark street. I pulled the Pontiac to the curb about half a block away so as not to block the ambulance, shoved my revolver into my belt, grabbed the bag with the wine and flowers, and ran quickly along the sidewalk. It was Lorrie's apartment all right.

A young squad-car cop was busy stringing yellow crime scene tape around the area to keep the gawkers at bay—not that there were likely to be many gawkers at that time of night. I pulled out my wallet and flashed it at him as if the flap contained something more serious than a shiny membership card for a video tape rental club.

"Detective Lombardo," I said as I ducked under the yellow line. To my surprise, he let me go. I went up the outside steps and up the inside steps and through the open door and into Lorrie's apartment where Sal Almonde's naked body was lying face down on Lorrie's white tiled kitchen floor. The entire back of his head was gone. Blood and brains and hair and assorted scraps of tissue had splattered the chairs and walls and the gleaming stainless electric stove. So much for cleanliness. The three live men in the room simply stood around staring. One of them was another squad car cop, a big, heavyset black guy who looked older and wiser than the young cop outside. Two were EMTs, white college boys in coveralls.

One of them had a goatee and was smoking a cigarette.

"So who the fuck are you?" the big cop said.

I didn't answer at first. In the other room, I could hear Lorrie's voice. She sounded hysterical. Two other cops were questioning her.

I started toward her, but the big cop got in my way.

"And where you think you're going?"

"I'm Pete Lombardo," I said. "That's my girlfriend in there."

The EMTs laughed a little. I hated them for that. The big cop frowned.

Lorrie was moving around frantically in the bedroom, and I could see she was wearing nothing but an old terrycloth bathrobe of mine that she let me keep in her closet so I'd have something to wear in the morning if I spent the night. "Lorrie," I said. I hadn't meant to say a word, but her name just spilled out.

She heard me and started to cry. "Oh, Pete," she said. "Oh, Peter."

"We gotta axe you some questions," the big cop said.

CHAPTER 33

When they found the revolver in my belt they took me to police headquarters before I had a chance to speak to Lorrie. I wasn't entirely sure I wanted to speak to her just yet anyway. I felt too damn betrayed by her to care if she were grieving, but I kept this to myself. That Sal Almonde was dead I felt pretty good about, but I kept this to myself too. Most cops aren't especially simple-minded, but a lot of them pretend to be, and I don't blame them. They get lied to by so many people with such regularity that preferring simple explanations for complex behavior becomes a way of coping.

A reaction formation, Lorrie would call it. But then finding complex explanations for simple behavior was the way Lorrie dealt with pain. She seemed to believe whole-heartedly that what was complex was true and hence forgivable, and I wasn't sure I believed that at all. There had probably been some kind of complicated daddy thing behind her sleeping with Sal Almonde, but frankly I didn't give a damn about any of that.

They put me in a one-way glass-walled room and ran a tape recorder as I told my story. I told it as best I could. I'd decided to visit my girlfriend. I'd seen the emergency vehicle and was worried about her, so I'd grabbed my gun and conned my way upstairs.

I was a private investigator and had a gun permit. Yes, I was shocked and dismayed to find to a naked dead man in her apartment. Yes, unfortunately I knew who the guy was. Yes, I could certainly account for my whereabouts at the probable time of the shooting. I told them about the Nomad Bar and about eating pie and ice cream at the State Street diner, and they sent someone over to check. Both Bill and Tessie the waitress backed up my story. In my car, I had a cash register tape with time and date for the flowers I'd bought, but while they were looking, they found my shotgun, which made them happy for a time, thinking they'd caught some kind of serial killer. But neither gun had been fired recently and both were registered and legal, and were also of the wrong caliber to match the single huge slug they dug out of Lorrie's wall.

Still, they bullied me for nearly six hours, asking the same simple questions over and over. Then they fed me an Egg-McMuffin breakfast and finally let me go at dawn. I had to bum a ride from the off-duty dispatcher to get back to Lorrie's street and collect my rental car. I didn't want to wait for a cab. Besides, what cabbie was going to stop for a guy carrying two guns—one of them a shot gun—plus a bottle of wine in a paper sack and a bouquet of wilted posies?

In all that time they hadn't let me see Lorrie, and I guessed she'd been grilled too, but when I got back to her street and saw her apartment light on, I had to ask myself what I wanted from her anyway. I decided it was better if I didn't see her just yet. I stopped at corner variety store to buy a cheap pocket knife with a corkscrew and uncorked the warm wine and took a big sloppy swig. What part of me wanted was to get in that moldy Pontiac and get as far away from Bridgewater as it would take me—to Florida maybe, but instead I finished the wine and slowly drove home.

I climbed the three flights of stairs to my apartment with a weariness that went bone deep. I'd been up all night long, and I had so much adrenaline, wine, and cop coffee in my system that my heartbeat was irregular and my stomach was sour. I wasn't even sure I could sleep, but I wanted to try. Or maybe I'd watch an early-morning test pattern on community-access TV. Stimulate those alpha brain waves. The last thing I wanted was an intruder in my apartment, but when I got to my door it was unlocked, and the lights were off. I could hear somebody moving around inside.

I went back to my car for my shotgun and loaded it with buck-shot shells from the glove compartment. Down the three flights of stairs and right back up again. I was breathing hard. If Almonde had sent a hit-man before he died, this might be my best and only opportunity to grease the bastard. I wasn't thinking especially clearly. When I got to the doorway I got down on my belly and moved to one side so I was partly screened by the heavy doorjamb, then I quietly reached up and turned the knob so that the door swung open and I saw a figure silhouetted in the half-light from a window.

"Die, Fucker," I said, and fired upward and somehow managed not only to miss the figure entirely but also to destroy the plaster-and-lath ceiling and send buckshot into the rafters and through the asphalt-shingled roof.

The sound of the shotgun blast echoed crazily in my ears and before it stopped echoing the figure turned to face me. I banged my forehead with my fist,

"I'm not sure how to take that, Peter," Lorrie said.

CHAPTER 34

She had a key to my apartment of course.

"I couldn't stay in my own place," Lorrie said. She brushed off plaster dust.

"Why come to me?" I asked, and sneezed.

"I didn't know where else to go. It was the middle of the night."

"Why didn't you tell me you were sleeping with Sal Almonde?"

"Oh, baby," she said. Suddenly, she was weeping again. She took a step toward me as if she meant for me to hug her. "You know how that kind of thing upsets you."

I didn't move. I wasn't feeling very forgiving just then, although I supposed she had a point.

"Who blew Almonde away?"

She began to sob in earnest. "I didn't see. He got out of bed to get a glass of water. I heard a bang. It wasn't loud—not like your gun. More like he'd bumped his knee in the dark. But he didn't come back. I went to see. I put my hand on his head, in the blood." She had fallen to her knees and was biting her hand and thrashing her head from side to side.

"Maybe a silencer," I said. "You can make a pretty good home-made one from a coffee can stuffed with plastic grocery bags. Especially if the barrel was right against his neck." I touched her shoulder, and she was suddenly all over me, almost toppling me backward, licking my face with her tongue.

I held her by the arms for a minute. "People always want to fuck after someone dies," I said. "It's some kind of monkey instinct."

It was a cruel thing to say, but it cooled her off a bit. "Yes," she said. "It's well documented."

I experienced a moment of stupid rage where I could almost see myself pounding Lorrie's head on the floor and ripping off her clothes and fucking her without a word and getting up and leaving her life forever. But thinking was one thing and doing was another. I stood there and rode my mood until it subsided and I began to feel a little guilty, but still I couldn't stop.

"Go take a cold shower," I said. "You're probably still full of Almonde's sperm."

Lorrie grimaced. "Sal always used condoms," she said matter-of-factly. "He insisted on safe sex."

"He would," I said. It was a little more than I wanted to know. "The bastard."

She was weeping softly again as she headed toward the shower.

Lorrie was scarcely out of my rust-stained tub when the sirens started and two brand-spanking-new cop cars pulled up downstairs. Then came the knock and the word "Police." The downstairs neighbors had called 911 about the noise. I opened the door and let them in. One of them was a big red-haired Irish cop and the other a wiry little Hispanic guy with acne and angled sideburns.

"So what's up, Doc? What happen to your ceiling?" the Hispanic cop said. He did a funky Bugs Bunny.

I tried to lie, of course, and said I hadn't realized the gun was loaded and that it had discharged by accident, but the cops had already been on the radio with headquarters and learned I'd recently been questioned in connection with another homicide.

"You were going wabbit hunting this morning maybe?"

I showed them my license and pistol permit.

They got on the radio to headquarters again.

"Maybe I shouldn't be talking to you?"

"Yeah, you got those funny rights," the Irish cop said, and asked me to turn as he kicked my legs apart and slipped the handcuffs on.

"Easy, Red," I said. "What's the charge?"

"Domestic violence," he said. "Or discharging a weapon within the Bridgewater city limits. Take your pick."

"It really *was* an accident," I said to Bugs, and by now I'd almost convinced myself that it had been. "Those charges will never stick."

"That's right," he said. He looked bored. "But, maybe you wouldn't have no accidents if you was sober."

The red haired cop turned to Lorrie. "He hurt you in any way?"

Lorrie shook her head. I felt sick deep in my guts, because I had, although not in the way he meant. Yet she'd lied to protect me. I felt a wave of tenderness for her, and now everything had turned to shit because the softness and forgiveness I was capable of seemed always to come too late.

"Be late tomorrow before he's arraigned and they release him," Red said. "Maybe by then you can find another boyfriend. Find yourself a brother. They treat you better."

Lorrie looked like she was about to cry again. He'd said exactly the worst thing. A psychic cop.

"Call Slade directly," I told her. "Try not to bother my father again if you can help it. But I want out—fast."

"Everybody wants out fast," the Hispanic cop said. "Out fast is the American way."

CHAPTER 35

The holding pen at the police station jail was full of drunks. Old drunks and young drunks. Black drunks and white drunks and even a Native American Indian drunk with a headband and dirty braids. Most of them were sleeping it off on cots with thin foam mattresses covered with clear plastic. A few were banging their heads on the walls or metal bars or hanging philosophically over the seat-less commode and puking when the spirit moved them. Every so often someone would miss the bowl. The smell right by the shitter was rancid and gagging—the smell of a social life experienced without illusion. It was even worse than the smell of that poisoned soil by the storage tank. A man puking his lungs out is incapable of dishonesty—or of honesty for that matter. He's something less than human. But after he's done, it all starts up again.

To kill time, we told our sad or erotic stories. Complex twisting tales of betrayal and loss told by men who sometimes didn't even have enough narrative sense to realize we didn't know the people they were talking about. They'd start right in. We'd pick up the pieces or not. A story told by a drunk with spittle on his lips to an utterly accepting audience.

When it was my turn, I decided to lay it out for them. I left out the real names. Otherwise I told my story in all its complexity. I'd expected pure acceptance because the other inmates had received nothing but nods and grins, but for some reason they challenged me.

"Let me get this straight," said a kid with barbed-wire tattoos on his wrists. "The old lady had a key to your apartment."

"Not the old lady, my girlfriend."

"But you said she was sleeping with this mob guy."

"Not the old lady, my girlfriend."

"But the old lady had the key?"

I shook my head. I'd thought I was being clear. Why they didn't understand me was a mystery. I began to try again, but then I stopped. Mid-sentence. Because I knew then without a doubt who had killed Jasper McLean.

CHAPTER 36

My father bailed me out again. Lorrie hadn't been able to contact Slade immediately—he was probably sleeping late, so she spent a few hours feeling frantic. Finally, she'd called my father, and he showed up immediately and paid another five-hundred dollars to guarantee I'd be in court—less because it was only a misdemeanor charge this time. They held me as long as they could, and then I signed papers and they let me go. Right away, Dad wanted to know about the holes in his roof, but I shook my head and asked him to drive me to the St. Christopher Hotel—which he did. I must have looked pretty bad because he didn't press me for details. He waited for me to speak. When I didn't, he turned on the radio. We listened to some Frank Sinatra. When he pulled up outside the St. Christopher, I opened the door and got out.

"Hey," he said. "You need any money?"

"I already paid for paid for the room," I said. "I'll call you."

"Be careful, son," he said. I felt a little sorry for him because suddenly he seemed real old. I wondered what it must be like to post bail for your adult son twice in the same week. I could imagine how I looked to him and what he must have thought when he learned I'd emptied a shotgun through the roof of the apartment he'd let me rent.

"Pop," I said. "I appreciate your sticking by me."

"I'd kind of been expecting another call," he said.

I didn't say anything to that, so. I slammed the car door. He pulled away from the curb, and I went up to my room. I was stupid with sorrow and weariness. I put the key in the lock but my door was open. Somehow I wasn't at all surprised to see Bosco in there, but I also had another visitor, a serious, dark-eyed Arab-looking guy with a scruffy beard, sitting patiently on my bed. He didn't look like a killer. In fact, the Arab guy had on an light gray suit and looked something like a lawyer—he was holding a yellow legal pad which was covered with some kind of cryptic handwriting. Fortunately, Geno wasn't anywhere to be found. I found that comforting, but even such comfort was cloaked in a kind of numbness.

"Petey, we're all gonna take us a little ride," Bosco said. He stood and took a gun from his shoulder holster.

"Is that necessary?" asked the stranger. He was frowning at Bosco's gun. "Can't we all talk here?"

I shook my head and smiled at Bosco. "It's not that I'm opposed to cement shoes as a fashion statement, but you and I both know that I didn't kill Sal Almonde. The cops already checked my whereabouts."

Bosco stared at me. His face was expressionless.

"You're the one in charge now, aren't you?" I said to Bosco. "Who's your gun-shy buddy?"

Bosco smiled and gestured with his chin, and the tall man rose and reluctantly checked me over to make sure I wasn't packing a weapon.

"My name is immaterial," the tall man said.

"Pleased to meet you, Mr. Immaterial," I said and stuck out my hand for him to shake. "Any friend of Bosco..."

He jerked backward. His aversion seemed so strong it was like he believed that I had cooties.

"Hey, guy, you ever watch football with the girls at the Ramada Inn?"

He grimaced and I knew I had his number. "The destruction of that hotel room was very, very foolish," he said. "We deny all involvement. And when we operate in the airports, we do so in cooperation with your federal authorities—to identify potential troublemakers, as it were. Fortunately, no one was injured."

"No skin off my ass."

"Indeed," he said. "But we have influence with the insurance company and with the parent corporation. All losses will be covered. The hotel will be rebuilt. A police investigation will be discouraged. Even in the early days, before 9/11, such tactics were frowned upon. Nowadays, we find such people an endless embarrassment." He tried smiling and corrected himself. "A public relations challenge."

"Yeah," I said, "but they're very convenient to have around. Just in case you need somebody kidnapped or killed."

When he didn't say anything more, I decided to press it. "Mutilating Greenwood in his own home was pretty dumb too. He left evidence in that upstairs closet that could have led the cops to your organization—if they wanted to be led, I mean."

"The desire for revenge may have caused some unknown party to act in an irrational manner. Some of our young women no doubt trusted to his medical professionalism. Dr. Greenwood obviously betrayed them."

"The good doctor liked to fuck young women while they were well sedated, and he kept their nipples as souvenirs," I said. "And he got paid pretty well for his out-patient plastic surgery. Except this one time he got so damn excited that he let one of his patients bleed to death while he was doing her. So he dumped her body in the parking garage, and nobody liked that much. Dr. Greenwood was a real sicko—he's better off dead."

"Look," Bosco said. "All this kinky Islamic-Greenwood shit has nothing to do with business." He paused and stared at Mr. Immaterial. "No offense."

Mr. Immaterial shrugged.

Bosco raised his eyebrows. "Almonde simply asked the Islamic Brightness people to keep a close eye on Lombardo here. Seeing as how they now got operatives at all the major airports and usually cooperate with the feds to provide security and keep things cool. This was obviously a rogue cadre. New-age Muslim fanatics. I guess they decided that our common interests had recently parted company."

"Makes perfect sense," I said. "Between my reporting Greenwood's body and my visiting Mrs. Mclean, they must have really thought I was somebody out to fuck them."

Mr. Immaterial still seemed pretty agitated. "The Islamic community is no more responsible for the actions of all its members than the Pope is responsible for the actions of all Catholics," he said.

"Like I said, so long as you keep me out of it, I really don't give a shit."

"You're in no position to give a shit," Bosco said. "And lay off the Pope," he told Mr. Immaterial.

"So your people have a vested interest in the railroads," I said. By way of the university's investment in Bridgewater Land. And that's probably why you bailed out the college—because you knew the potential value of some old stock certificates they held in their endowment portfolio, even if they didn't understand what it was worth."

Mr. Immaterial walked to the tiny sink to turn on the water to make some white noise before he spoke.

"We don't consider profit to be crime. We're certainly unapologetically entrepreneurial in our orientation. There's also an important spiritual dimension."

"How about murder for profit?" I said. "Is that part of the liturgy?"

"Yeah," Bosco said. "Maybe we should talk some after all. If Lombardo didn't kill Almonde, who did?"

"You'd like it to be me," I said.

Bosco let that ride. "You're tailor-made," he said. "Her jealous lover did it."

"How about this as motivation: Almonde was willing to double-cross both Islamic Brightness and the city. As a co-owner of that right-of-way, he could work with the mayor and squeeze the railroads. Or he could play both ends against the middle. As owner of that spur line, he could offer the railroads a better deal—a way to run their trains through Bridgewater without leasing from Bridgewater Land."

"So?" he said calmly.

"You're already talking like a man in charge," I said. "You need to think like one."

"You're alleging that our people killed Mr. Almonde?" asked Mr. Immaterial.

"Fuck, for all I know the city cops killed him. Maybe they were looking forward to a raise as their share of the railroad money."

"That's pretty far out," said Bosco. "The deal wasn't public knowledge."

"Mayor Silverstone was all over it. He beat me to the records. The cops are his private army. He would have been deeply upset when he discovered that Almonde was prepared to offer the freight lines an alternative route. And no wonder Big John Marr was pissed when he found out that I made that call about Greenwood. He wanted to keep things simple and disconnected, and some of those rookie vice cops are probably dumb and idealistic enough to jump at the chance to clean up Dodge."

"So you're saying the mayor of Bridgewater had the police kill Sal Almonde?" asked Mr. Immaterial. "Not necessarily," I said. "I'm saying it's a light-hearted murder mystery. And that maybe you need to go hire yourself a private detective to investigate."

"So you don't actually know shit?"

"Since when did knowing anything become my business?"

"Under the circumstances, I'd speculate," Bosco said.

"For free?"

Bosco waved his gun at me. "None of us appreciated that stunt with the Hell's Angels."

I took a deep breath. "As a matter of fact, there's one individual who could profit immediately from Sal Almonde's death—assuming, of course that he was less greedy than Almonde and ready to make nice with the other co-owners of Bridgewater Land."

Bosco smiled. "Now you're saying I did it?"

"Actually, I tried that theory out on about twenty drunks in lock-up a few hours ago. They didn't have much trouble. In a couple of days they'll be telling it all over town."

Bosco cocked his gun.

I smiled. "Kill me, and the boys in Atlantic City will decide those ugly rumors are true. Especially if they realize the cops checked out my alibi and found it sound. If there's anything your parent organization values, it's loyalty. You want to run Almonde's operation? They got to trust you. Right now the big Atlantic City bosses might hear rumors and suspect something, but they got no proof. They'll likely give you the benefit of the doubt and leave it to you to seek proper vengeance for Almonde—if and when you can figure out who offed him. After all, this is your territory now. But if I get dead right away, and it doesn't check out, they'll start looking elsewhere. And so will the SBI, by the way, because I've made provision to mail them my information posthumously. So basically, it's cheaper and simpler to keep me alive if you want to screw the railroads."

Bosco and Mr. Immaterial looked at one another.

"What's all that silence worth to you?" Bosco asked.

"Nothing," I said. "What's good for Almonde Enterprises and the good folks at Islamic Brightness is good for the people of Bridgewater. I'd just like you to call Mayor Silverstone and the cops and tell everybody we're square. Otherwise I've got all this shit documented and ready to go public, and you'd need to hire yourself an entire army of spin doctors to deal with the bad publicity."

Bosco laughed. "You're all right, Lombardo. You're one crazy motherfucker, but basically you're all right."

"Does Geno know anything?" I said.

He laughed derisively. "Geno," he said, "is Geno."

"So how much did the old lady pay you to do what you'd do for free?" I asked.

"What?" Bosco seemed incredulous. "You're saying I'm working for the old lady?"

"Oh," I said. "So I guess I got that part wrong."

"You got it all wrong. I didn't kill Sal Almonde." He frowned at me. He was thinking hard and he wasn't used to it.

"If you say so," I said. "Maybe it was Hiram Silverstone's people after all. I keep seeing connections where there aren't any."

"I'll let you get some sleep," Bosco said.

"Nighty night," I said. I pulled back a worn sheet and climbed into bed. "Lock the door on your way out."

For a moment I thought I'd pushed Bosco too far, that he'd put a cartridge through my brain just to stop my wisecracks, but he was already shouldering the burden of leadership and actually did as I asked.

I fell back on the bed and counted the tiny cracks in the water-stained brown ceiling. In a minute I was asleep.

CHAPTER 37

I had a funny dream. A dream I finally remembered. A dream about my mother. It had been so long I didn't think I recalled what she looked like, but in my dream it all came back. She was standing with me by the front door of our house—not the one my father lived in now but the smaller wood-framed duplex we had lived in when I was a kid. It was winter. There'd been a foot or two of snow the night before. She had on a long cloth coat with a fur collar. I was wearing a snowsuit and red mittens and black rubber boots with metal buckles. I was having trouble walking because the snow suit was bulky and the drifts were very high. So I was standing by my mother's side. My father had a camera and he was trying to take our picture. My mother was laughing and held her hand up before her face.

"Let me shoot you," my father said.

She laughed and giggled like a teenager, and back then she was only a few years older than that. I watched as he clicked the shutter once and turned the crank handle to advance the film.

"You moved," he said.

She smiled again, but somehow it wasn't funny.

"I'm only trying to get off a single goddamn shot!" he said.

She frowned and took her hand away. I could suddenly see her face and remember what she looked like. How soft her body and features were. Her eyelashes were long and looked wet with falling snow.

"You spoil everything, David," she said, "because you don't know how to simply be." She turned toward the house and took my arm to pull me after her.

"Leave him," my father said.

"I'm leaving you," she said.

He lifted the camera and aimed and clicked as she turned, so that I wasn't sure he'd caught her face or back or simply captured a blur.

She pulled on my arm, again.

"Don't take the boy," my father said. "I've only got one son."

"You don't know what love is, David," my mother said.

"I'd kill for him," my father said.

"Exactly," she said. And when she turned again, it wasn't to the house but to the old Bridgewater train station. I saw her face in the train window as the coach-car was pulling away.

I woke with a start, got out of bed without turning on the light, dressed in the predawn darkness, and left the room without ever turning the light on. Outside the St. Christopher Hotel, the air was cold and clear as it is sometimes, even in Bridgewater, before dawn. I walked three blocks to the bus station and found a cab and gave the cabbie my father's address. The driver was a big taciturn Slovak who sipped coffee as he drove, and we zipped over to Park Avenue where we could head north without traffic. He pulled to the curb in front of my father's house. I paid him in cash and he left me there in silence. It was still pretty early. Even the birds weren't sounding off yet. I found a spare key to the back door under a rock by the whiskey barrel planter on the deck and let myself in as quietly as I could and turned off that alarm system I'd installed, although I knew there wasn't a chance in hell it would work as it should. I felt like a cat burglar as I crept down the hallway to the storage closet and fumbled in the darkness of unworn winter coats and checked the far corner for his old Army rifle. Of course, it wasn't there.

"Boo," my father said.

I jumped a foot and nearly fouled my pants. "Heart attacks run in the family," I said.

"Sal Almonde was always a no-good piece of shit," he said. "I couldn't have him killing you. And as for that little colored girl..."

"I'm glad you got rid of that old rifle, Pop," I said. "An unregistered weapon isn't something a law-abiding citizen ought to have lying around."

"A thing like that would be better at the bottom of Long Island Sound," he said, and headed back into his bedroom.

I went down to the kitchen, put hot water in a mug and the mug in the microwave. When it beeped I took it out and stirred in some instant decaf. It was all I could find. Then I rubbed my eyes and drank the coffee and waited. I could hear a shower starting upstairs. I let myself out again before my father came down to breakfast.

CHAPTER 38

I wasn't quite ready to return my rental car or deal with my Escort, so I swung by the University to see Mrs. McLean. I walked up the flagstone path and rang the bell. The gargoyle on the door was as repulsive as ever. She opened the door immediately and swung it wide, but seemed astonished to see me. I pushed past her into the foyer.

"I feared you might have become a victim of foul play, Mr. Lombardo," she said softly.

"Sorry to disappoint."

She didn't say anything to that, but she followed me back to her sitting room. The faded upholstery looked even more worn, if that were possible, but she'd bought herself a new TV—one of those flat, wide-screen plasma jobs.

"Better sit down," I said, and she did.

"Do you wish to report?"

"Geno did it," I lied. "Not me."

"Did what?"

"Bumped Almonde."

I could tell she was interested, but I wanted to torture her a bit. She hesitated. "And who, pray tell, is Geno?"

"One of Almonde's trusted associates. He wanted a bigger piece of the pie."

"These hooligans are no doubt quite horrible people, Mr.

Lombardo."

"He must have taken lessons," I said.

"I'm not sure I follow your thinking today."

"There's another matter. Your husband's death. Sal Almonde supplied the narcotic. You administered it. You put him behind the wheel. You started the car and locked the garage and went to bed. That's why he didn't have his garage keys."

She seemed visibly agitated. "Preposterous," she said.

"Yeah," I said.

"And my motive?"

"Sordid," I said. "Fifty years ago you were sleeping with Sal Almonde."

She didn't even seem surprised I knew. "I loved him," she said. "I loved the man."

"Fuck that," I said. "Sal Almonde was your boy-toy. You were what—ten or fifteen years older than him?"

"He already had a family. A wife and young children. He made the honorable choice."

"Yeah," I said. "Only you didn't poison your husband soon enough. Talk about strange bedfellows. McLean gave the railroads a fifty-year lease. Almonde was using you, but it didn't work. So once the lease was signed, he dumped you."

"Sal was in love with me," she said. "He was. You wouldn't understand such passion."

"If you say so, old lady. Even back then you were an old lady to him."

She ignored the jab. "He made the honorable choice. He stayed with his wife and family."

"So you kept quiet for fifty years. Until you found out he was screwing Lorrie."

She closed her eyes and breathed deeply for a while. It was almost as if she'd gone to sleep.

"Lorrie was right to love him. Who wouldn't love a man like that?"

"One in a million," I said.

"Irony masks impotence, Mr. Lombardo, as I told you once before."

"I do my best," I said.

"But that Sal should love her. That I could not tolerate. I deserved him. I deserved his love."

"And justice ain't easy to come by," I said. "So you hired me to make him sweat. You figured he'd probably threaten me, and maybe you'd turn him in—if I turned up dead. You could hold that over him because you could provide the cops with a simple motive for hatred between us—jealousy. Because Lorrie was sleeping with both Almonde and me and you knew it. Besides which—you knew Lorrie was infatuated with Almonde, and he couldn't bring up the McLean connection as an alternate motive without implicating himself in another murder."

She gave me a disapproving look. "Lorrie was not infatuated."

"Maybe," I said. "That's for her to say. Hell, maybe I'll ask her again to marry me—that is if she'll even talk to me. But how about the rest of it?"

Then she smiled. A warm sly smile. "Well, Mr. Lombardo, perhaps I underestimated you. You seem to be a rather competent detective after all. Except, of course, about these matters of the heart."

"So that's why he tried to scare me off. You told him that I was coming after him, didn't you? You told him I knew about Jasper McLean's murder."

She nodded. "I'll deny all this, of course."

"And when he didn't kill me right away, you ordered the exhumation to torque the bolts a bit?"

"I deeply regret using you," she said. "But my options were rather limited, and I wanted only the justice that was my due."

"Wasn't exhumation sort of dangerous? Seeing as how you and Almonde could both be implicated?"

"The wheels of legal recourse turn very slowly, Mr. Lombardo— at least for those with sufficiently deep pockets to keep well-compensated lawyers filing motions for delays. It could take many decades to convict me—if ever—and even longer to exhaust my opportunities to appeal. Meanwhile, posing no risk of flight, my aging body would remain at large."

"Well, Sal Almonde is dogmeat," I said. "Is that justice enough?"

She nodded and twisted her hands together like Lady Macbeth.

"And what about Jasper McLean? He loved you."

She laughed, a low, bitter laugh. "He was a socialist. He loved everybody."

"Yeah, and sooner or later Islamic Brightness will have this house and his money."

"Will you go to the police?" she asked.

I gave her a look. "I'll leave it to the cops to figure out—which they won't. For all I know, things will work for the best. With the profits from that lucrative new railroad lease swelling the city coffers, they might open up the public library forty hours a week and pick up all the garbage. The good citizens of Bridgewater will appreciate that."

"Yes," she said, "I suppose they will."

"Jasper McLean's legacy," I said.

"Then our business is concluded, Mr. Lombardo?" She stood up slowly, tottering on her ivory cane.

"Sure," I said. "Except that I want an extra twenty-thousand bucks."

Her eyebrows went up. "Extortion, Mr. Lombardo? Frankly, I'm surprised."

"I spent your retainer and I got holes in a roof to fix. I need to buy myself a smelly Pontiac before it snows. I need a vacation in Florida so I can send some alligator postcards. I need to return some bail money in case I decide to skip town. And I need to pay off about twenty Hell's Angels before they decide I stiffed them."

She reached for her checkbook and pen, her movements so slow and deliberate they seemed almost ceremonial. "You have some very strange needs, Mr. Lombardo."

"Yeah," I said, "I do."

About the Author

Michael Colonnese has worked as an advertising copywriter, an organic farmer, a chemical salesman, a real estate agent, a Pinkerton guard, and a soundman and editor for a documentary film company. He holds a Ph.D. from Binghamton University, and currently lives in Fayetteville, NC, where he directs the Creative Writing Program at Methodist University and serves as managing editor for Longleaf Press.

LaVergne, TN USA
16 October 2010
201078LV00002B/3/P